*FAST RIDE WITH THE TOP DOWN*

# FAST RIDE WITH THE TOP DOWN

A NOVEL
by Harper Grey

**alyson books**

LOS ANGELES • NEW YORK

Manufactured in the United States of America.
Printed on acid-free paper.

This trade paperback is published by Alyson Publications Inc.,
P.O. Box 4371, Los Angeles, California 90078-4371.

Also published in cloth by Alyson Publications
First edition: June 1996
First paperback printing: July 1997

01 00 99 98 97    10 9 8 7 6 5 4 3 2 1

ISBN 1-55583-416-7

**Library of Congress Cataloging-in-Publication Data**
Grey, Harper.
    Fast ride with the top down / a novel by Harper Grey. — 1st ed.
    ISBN 1-55583-370-5 (cloth); 1-55583-416-7 (pbk)
    I. Title.
PS3557.R4817F37  1996
813'.54—dc20                              96-7367  CIP

Cover design by Wayne DeSelle.

For Peggy Turk

L acy Blackwood was orphaned at fourteen. Her parents died in a fall from a roller coaster. This happened on Key West, where the family spent its winters.

The amusement park was a transient affair, jerry-built for a week's stay on a vacant patch out by the airport. Clownland. All the ride operators and booth men were thematically suited up, but desultorily—ruffled collars lying limp against stained T-shirts, greasepaint with razor stubble poking through.

The night of the accident, the place had been hired out for a black-tie benefit. Mid-sixties, upper-class recherché—the sort of thing the young and moneyed did for reverse chic before they discovered country bars and deco diners.

Lacy's parents were only in their thirties. The drinking had only gotten to a place that made them seem slightly more celebratory than everyone else, contentiousness giving their marriage a light cutting edge. Never to come were the bruises and boorishness, the too-loud scenes in quiet restaurants, the weepy collapses at parties, the mornings after of unremembered insults and lost automobiles. They would never have

1

the chance to begin their long and tiresome decline. Their fall froze them in their most glamorous moment, suspended them forever in an aspic of stylishness and hilarity.

The accident happened around nine-thirty at night. Lacy assumed that since they were generally drunk from early afternoon on, this was what was behind it all. No one said anything about this, of course. At least not to her or her brother, Franco. Just *What a lovely couple, nipped in their prime, such a tragedy.*

"No one else was hurt, did you notice?" Lacy said to Franco. "No one said anything about the ride breaking down. They probably stood up. I bet they just unhooked the bar and stood up." In her imagination, they had fallen silent through the wet night air, landed bloodless on the sand and sea grass. It wasn't until well into Lacy's adulthood that her Aunt Helen corrected this impression.

A teary moment. "I've never been able to think directly about it," Helen had said. "In the end, your father winding up in all that plush."

"Slush?"

"No. A booth, some kind of game. You know. There's a miniature steam shovel. You pick up stuffed animals. That's where he landed, on a pile of terrible prizes. The little shovel was picking at him." She stopped. "I'm being stupidly upsetting. I'm sorry."

"Don't tell Franco," Lacy said. She knew that her brother had, over the years, worked out an elegant version of the event. Something like Cole Porter being crushed beneath his polo pony, Isadora Duncan strangled as her scarf caught in the spokes of her Bugatti. Something that wouldn't be needing a banana peel.

I t's early evening. Lacy is on the old yellow sofa in her studio reading some letters of Virginia Woolf. She loves how, in one letter, Virginia Woolf is a dignified literary personage, then in the next, to her girlfriend, is "Yr Potto."

She places the open book flat on her stomach while she imagines what it must have been like to live like V. Woolf in a chilled gray place. A country with the climate of a refrigerator lettuce keeper. Someplace where you'd always have to work at taking the edge off, with big cups of tea and gas fireplaces. Long sweaters.

Instead of on this island, where the weather is cotton and pastel. You slip into it in the morning as you slip out of sleep. Easy, like everything around here. Sometimes all the easiness sets Lacy's nerves flapping around like power lines during a storm.

The phone rings. She lies still, letting the machine pick up. After her message, there's a beep, then Franco. He took the car half an hour ago to drive over to the supermarket to get them something Stouffery for dinner.

She could answer. He knows she's here, listening, but instead, she lets him talk to the tape. Sometimes she needs the filter.

"I'm sort of stuck," he says.

He's waiting at the front of the store when she gets there, sitting on the bags in a charcoal briquet display, next to a sale bin of Spanish olives. The store has some futuristic lighting that makes tomatoes look better and people look worse. Franco's skin color in here is that of an alien from some suburban galaxy doing a pretty good, but not perfect job of impersonating a human.

He's wearing clerical clothing. Casuals, though—not a cassock or any of the more dramatic stuff (capes, miters) that he orders from ecclesiastical catalogs. Just black pants and shirt. He has left off the Roman collar and opened the shirt a couple of buttons, rolled the long sleeves up in a bunchy way, and so he doesn't look particularly religious. Given how thin he is and how green in this light and how agitated, he looks more like a junkie than a priest.

He motions her to follow him and takes her back to the pop section.

"You see. Now they've got Pepsi and Diet Pepsi and Pepsi Free. And Diet Pepsi Free. I think a lot of people would get stuck."

"Here's the store brand." She pulls down a can. "It's just Cola. It's probably okay. Just stick with this."

He can't even go into the 31 Flavors. He becomes magnetized, especially by new and improved products, anything extra-strength or lite, anything endorsed by a marginal celebrity. He loves commercials, draws metaphor off them. "Just do it," he'll say when a jogger passes them on the street. Or "Like a rock" as he pats the fender of a truck in a parking lot. There's a lot of irony to this, of course, but that's not quite all of it. If he were truly detached, he wouldn't need to be rescued from overstimulation in the Winn-Dixie.

Every year, just after Christmas, Lacy's family would go to Key West. With the trunk stuffed, they'd set out in the Continental, a massive, squared-off car that looked more like a major appliance than an automobile. It was even a kitcheny color—loden green. They usually planned to leave early in the morning, but inevitably Lacy's parents got so anxious they started off the night before. All this did was give them a thin illusion of momentum. Which lasted until they got to the far south side of Chicago, at which point they would pull into a motel.

In those pre-interstate days of two- and three-lane highways, the trip might take the average driver four days. It took Lacy's family longer. How much longer depended partly on how many times they got lost. Lacy's mother was a terrible navigator. She was often on the wrong page of the AAA TripTik; she would have the right directions for getting them through Georgia, but when they were only as far as Tennessee.

Then, too, whole afternoons were often given over to sights with persuasive billboards. Rock gardens. Lookout points from which you could see four states at once. Sometimes the attraction was just a roadside lot offering rides on ponies so mangy that they looked like small humpless camels. Once they stayed four days outside Knoxville at a motel attached to a roller rink where Tom Blackwood had become taken with the notion of the family that skates together.

While Lacy enjoyed particular pony-ride and cavern and roller-rink moments, the uncertain tenor of these trips led her to fantasies of traveling by Greyhound, with a destination sign on the front and a uniformed driver firmly gripping the wheel, a pocket of scheduled stops between here and there. She was always relieved when they finally reached Key West.

She and Franco didn't have to go to school down south; they brought their books along, then left them in the trunk of the car. The nuns in Lake Forest never really checked up on whether they'd done the coursework, so, in lieu of studying, they passed their days at the Casa Marina beach, where their parents had a cabana and an understanding with the bartender.

It was during these winters that Lacy learned the butterfly, and Franco developed a morbid fascination with man-o'-wars. Their mother told him about a boy who had died when one crawled onto his chest.

Lacy's mother had come into adulthood expecting a life filled with event. She eloped with Tom Blackwood when she was nineteen; soon she had two children and a Tudor house on the tame plains of Chicago's north shore, where all the snags were smoothed away—automatic sprinklers sunk in the lawns, potpourri sacks nestled in the drawers, *Reader's Digest* condensed books on the shelves. Despite these unpromising surroundings, she led an inner life of high adventure and pulled her family onto her raft even as it headed toward the rapids, the white water waiting just around the next bend.

If in the spring or fall, a tornado watch was announced, a funnel having been sighted outside Benton Harbor or

Madison, she would herd the family down to the basement and pass around M&Ms and Cokes, keeping a sharp ear to the portable radio for bulletins. She encouraged Lacy and Franco to take lifesaving and first-aid courses and to become crossing guards at school.

"Look," she'd say, pointing to a photo in the *Tribune*. "Here's a little boy who towed his brother two miles to shore. Through rapids. You have to always be ready with your cross-chest carry."

This left Lacy with a legacy of overpreparedness. Coming into her own adulthood, she had to face the disappointing realization that life probably wasn't going to happen in Technicolor. Franco simply chose not to take delivery on this deflating information.

He was his mother's dreamchild. He confessed every Saturday. If he forgot a sin, he went back—often two or three times in an afternoon. For double coverage, he wore both a scapular and a Miraculous Medal. He was head altar boy in the parish, lead in the school May Crowning. He was the favorite of the nuns and adored them in return. He wanted to be a nun until Lacy explained to him that this wasn't really an option.

It was late into grade school that he began customizing Catholicism to his own specs. He started celebrating his own masses: for high ones, he wore robes over robes to get a chasuble effect. For low ones, he designed what he called a "sports chaz," a satin baseball jacket with IHS in iron-on tape across the back. He built an altar against one wall of his bedroom; in it he installed a cigar box containing a third-class relic of Saint Sebastian, a tee used by Arnold Palmer in a Masters tournament, and a 45 of Chuck Berry's "Nadine."

Lacy was his acolyte. Before mass she would kneel in front of his slightly open closet door while he sat inside between the hanging folds of chino and madras. In preparation for receiving communion, a Necco wafer, she would whisper made-up mortal sins—doubting the mysteries of faith, allowing herself despair.

Then Franco started becoming more serious about these rituals, which in turn became less derivative, more idiosyncratic. This departure started after their parents died. Cutting their faces out of snapshots, he glued them over the faces of his Mary and Joseph statues, installing them in his iconography as Saint Tom and Saint Fran, Patrons of Fun.

He started stealing real communion wafers, holding the host in his mouth until he got back to his pew, then dropping it off his tongue into a matchbox to bring it home. The first one he put into his Roy Orbison monstrance, which he had shaped out of crushed aluminum foil, the host enclosed between two sunglass lenses.

"Why don't you get out of the house more?" Lacy urged. "Get a paper route or something?"

She was drifting off. She had other things to do. She'd started painting, joined the swim team at school. She had no interest in spending more of her Saturday afternoons in an incense-choked bedroom.

He prayed end-to-end novenas for her return.

"You're my lost sheep," he told her.

Lacy didn't know what to think. At times she thought it might be possible, as he said, that Christ's teachings could be interpreted in many ways. Sometimes she could even be persuaded on individual points. That John Lennon was God's special messenger to the modern world; that golf, especially putting, was a form of prayer.

In other, longer moments away from him, though, it seemed pretty likely that her brother was a lunatic.

On good days like this one, Lacy paints straight through, from after breakfast until she loses her light in the late afternoon. She loves her work.

It's a love of many aspects: She has strong visual takes, and painting gives her a way to lay them out. She loves the paints themselves, their primary smell, loves how even after such a long time, so many years, she can still mix a color she has never seen before.

She loves the solid planes and hard boundaries of the medium. So much of everything else in life is abstract and vaporous, the grounds on which choices can be made too susceptible to shifting. But canvas can be stretched onto precise rectangles; colors fall along a single spectrum; good brushes perform faithfully for a long time.

Laws of perspective and foreshortening, light and shadow, while violable, are always there to fall back on. Within this reasonable universe, she can fly without fear of losing her footing.

Lacy doesn't think of herself as a real artist, though. She could kid herself; she has gotten a small fellowship, had a summer's residency at an artists' colony. Her work gets hung in a Duval Street gallery, but this is the sort of place that also sells polished driftwood "sculptures" and a line of gay Hummel-like figurines. She's just a painter; her paintings are hung because they sell, and they sell because they're well-executed and directly address posterish themes. They have subjects that people don't mind thinking about again each time they pass the sofa wall in their living room.

There are practical considerations behind doing this sort of work. She has to support herself, and mostly support Franco. (He brings in very little, doing translations of instructions for toys and gadgets made in other, chiefly Asian, countries.) But really, if she had the true grit for suffering she could be ruthless, whittle their lifestyle to the bone. Buy at Bucky's Caseload Groceries. Frequent the public library more. Reuse foil. Buy time for making real art.

She used to do this. For years, she was working on a series of paintings she never showed anyone. Lately, she has stopped working on these. She's aware that she's holding back. Trying not to risk anything, or surprise herself.

Today she's working on the next to last in a group of paintings—abstractions of modern myths. The series before this was based in Floridian underside. Nightshade interiors. Mirrored bedrooms of tootsies. Ashtrays propping lipsticked, unfiltered, smokeless cigarettes. Explicit weapons and implicit victims.

Harry Windsor, who owns the gallery on Duval and reps Lacy, hung a few of these in a group show last year. He considers Lacy an "artist of promise." Artists of promise get their work hung in group shows. Individual shows are reserved for artists who've arrived, or whom Harry thinks he can make arrive.

Lacy is still a station or two down the track.

When they were young, Lacy and Franco tried to figure things out from television. Watching dramas and comedies of family life, they came to see America as a foreign country where fathers disappeared in the morning, launched on balanced breakfasts and wifely kisses at the door, then reappeared at dinnertime, suiting down to elbow-patched jackets for serious newspaper reading, helping with homework and dispensing considered advice.

Mothers were encapsuled in kitchens, wore freshly pressed housedresses, baked and frosted an endless assault of cupcakes. Settled disputes with placid equanimity.

Everyone slept in single beds and pajamas, over which they put on robes whenever they left their rooms—even to go downstairs in the middle of the night, even to confront burglars.

Kids were up to mischief, but fundamentally good. They had lots of friends.

Not Lacy and Franco, who made friends uneasily. Early on, it became clear that most kids lived in this other America. They lived in households that acknowledged weekdays and weekends, school years and summer vacations, observed national holidays and some kind of Standard Time—while Lacy and Franco inhabited a territory where there were no linchpins in a day, like dinner, or in a year, like birthdays.

Neither of their parents worked. There was money on both sides to run through, which they did with élan.

By the time they died, there was almost nothing left but the houses in Key West and Lake Forest—the closets filled with custom putters, drawers stacked with hand-monogrammed shirts. If they hadn't fallen from the roller coaster, they would have surely plummeted headlong over the sheer drop created by their carelessness. In the end, they made living like there was no tomorrow pay off.

Their life, while they were living it, was not one into which Lacy and Franco could easily bring anyone. There was too much that would require explanation. If they were going to come home from school at three in the afternoon to find their parents having a candlelight dinner in silk pajamas, this was a discovery best made unaccompanied by outsiders.

Sometimes, though, for a little while or in a certain aspect, things would start to seem regular, normal. For instance, one day in the spring of the year they died, their parents got a dog, which some guy they met in a bar sold to them out of his car for three dollars. The guy called her a pup, which they all went along with, taking her white muzzle for an eccentricity of breed.

When they took her to the vet, he told them she was of several breeds and already middle-aged—seven, maybe eight years old. They never got together on naming her. Everyone called her something different. Happy. Lad. Rover. Franco called her Tweetie.

She came with an accumulation of odd behaviors. She often peed in the vicinity of the toilet, as though someone had put her through some avant garde form of housebreaking, but only gotten halfway with it. She suffered from an uncontrollable rivalry with, or hatred of, cars—it was hard to tell which—and would chase after them as they passed the house. Mostly just for a few yards or down to the end of the block, but sometimes for miles.

These last bouts left the cars' passengers shaken and Lacy's family out for hours tracking the dog down. They were worried she'd get picked up by the police and taken to the pound, where Franco assured everyone they would put her in "the chamber." Each time they finally found her, she would look around at all of them in bewilderment, like the librarian with multiple personalities who finds she has just spent the past two days and a thousand dollars on a nightclub spree in San Juan. Then, with exhausted relief, would fall asleep for a day.

They tried to get the dog to sleep outside. They built a doghouse, put an old blanket inside. Lacy ran extension cords down from her bedroom and put a radio in there to keep the dog company at night. It was no good. As soon as the dog had been locked outside the screen door at night, she would begin to bay—wildly, relentlessly, like a keener at a wake in some primitive time and place.

And so their father would go out and sleep in his striped boxer shorts on a chaise in the backyard with the dog snug between his arm and bare chest. While Stevie Wonder and Gladys Knight drifted out softly from the doghouse radio.

A larger problem was that the dog liked to bite Howard Maver, who lived next door. No one knew why; there didn't seem to be anything especially provocative about him. He was a quiet kid. He even liked the dog—until she started biting him.

The first time she bit him there was a trip to the hospital for Howard, a trip to the vet for the dog, and much over-politeness on the parts of both sets of neighbors. The second time, there was an extremely unpleasant scene when Howard's father, also Howard, came over to discuss the situation. It was unfortunate that, at that moment, Tom Blackwood and the dog were dancing out on the patio. The dog was not a terrific dancer; all she did was hop around sideways in an incoherent way, totally off the beat. But she enjoyed herself, so they all humored her.

The sight of Tom Blackwood dancing with the dog that had twice bitten his child drove Howard Senior—a young investments analyst, who had once lectured Franco on the importance of keeping shoes on shoe trees—into brief psychotic break. The police were called.

This enraged Tom Blackwood, who chose to take this as an attack not only on his dog but on his self-image as a dad, the head of a household. After decking one of the cops with a lucky surprise punch, he was taken away in a squad car. Later that night, when he was brought back in his lawyer's Mercedes, he seemed to have sobered up but was still offering large and inappropriate solutions to the problem. They would have to put the house on the market, he said, and move some place where the dog was properly appreciated.

The next day, Lacy tacked a notice on the bulletin board in the Jewel. By the weekend they had found the dog a new home with an old lady from Rogers Park who had been robbed of two televisions in the past year. She had had dogs before, and she seemed to like this one right off. Lacy took pictures of them together in front of the house with her Kodak Brownie.

She loved the dog but knew she would be far less nervous without her around to draw the neighbors' attention to the problems. The Problems.

Tom and Frances Blackwood mourned the loss of the dog hugely. They stood on the front lawn and waved as the old lady drove off. The dog, busy barking at a guy pushing an electric mower, didn't notice.

Lacy's parents went inside and spent the night toasting the dog and ultimately all dogs. They sang "Old Shep" and "How Much Is That Doggie in the Window?"—adding gin and lime juice to fact, coming up with instant myth.

Every morning, straight out of bed, Lacy bikes out to Simonton, past the frame guesthouses—white with green trim, yellow with white—where no one has yet awakened to his complimentary quiche and tequila sunrise. Everything's quiet this early; no one's out. The sidewalks are clear enough for the palmetto bugs to frisk around fearlessly. They don't have to pretend to be fallen leaves.

She pedals past the motels with their humming ice machines and already-weary chambermaids pushing carts filled with fresh sheets and toilet-seat tapes and plastic cups. She cuts over on United and heads out to the city pool. It's a forgotten place out of a dreamscape, ancient and crumbling like a relic of some previous swimming civilization. The entrance is through dank cement catacombs of unused lockers and changing rooms, dripping showers, walls perspiring with flaking paint.

The pool itself sits above ground, circled by a sagging chain-link fence. It's in such a state of neglect that the last long-ago color is worn away in vast uneven patches exposing even longer-ago shades of aquamarine. The overall effect is a set for a party of circus clowns and debutantes, a Fellini out-take.

Lacy swims a mile here every day. She climbs the high platform and stands briefly in the center of a great and extremely specific fear. Then she pushes will against flesh and dives. Clearing the nerves.

After her swim she meets Franco for breakfast at Huey's, a snack shop that has never, in Lacy's time, had a Huey in evidence. Today she has a muffin and tea; Franco orders French toast, bacon, hash browns, coffee with cream, a special he calls the Coronary Occlusion. While he waits for it to arrive, he reads his breviary. Lacy ogles a couple of guys having breakfast in the back booth, or rather not having breakfast in the back booth. They're too preoccupied with, by turns, looking at each other and not being able to look at each other. Drinking coffee is about all the peripheral activity they can manage. They've just showered, their hair is still damp with fresh comb tracks. Their shirts, just shaken out of their suitcases, are creased with large squares. Desire surfaces in Lacy. She wants this kind of voltage.

She likes watching gay guys around the island. Sometimes they're in love, but even if they're not, they're very good at lust. Even more, she enjoys watching the women. They don't flaunt it so much as the guys. They're unadvertised specials. They sit over fettucine in Antonia's or on the stone edge of Mallory docks at sunset, looking like friends since music camp or volunteers from the same crisis hotline, but not really. The interest level is too high, the laughter too nerved-up; the eye contact has a locked-in quality with no peripheral glances. Nothing on the periphery could be of more interest. You wouldn't notice any of this unless you were looking for it, but when you do, it comes up like lemon juice script on paper held over a flame. Lacy notices it a lot.

She forces herself to break off staring at the back booth and looks the other way. There's another point of interest: a bag lady, except she only has one bag and it's an okay black vinyl carryall. It's the only thing about her that is okay, though. She's wearing a maroon velvet evening gown that has been cut, but not hemmed, at the knee. Her hair is of an astounding length. It's pulled up into a nest of tangles at the base of her neck, caught in one of those heavy, triangular dime-store nets used to bind up roller sets in beauty salons of the sixties. She has an odd face—old, but with no past to it. Like the faces of children in places where life is especially hard. It's hard to figure her age. She could be anywhere from sixty on.

She's having an order of toast, which she's spreading with jam, syrup, then sugar from a counter container. She drinks the coffee halfway down, fills it to the top with cream, and drinks this. Lacy wonders what she'll do next.

What she does next is slide the plate over from the place next to her. The guy who just left has abandoned it with most of his potatoes still intact. After fastidiously removing the wad of gum he parked on the rim of the plate, she polishes them off.

Noticing she's being noticed, she smiles widely at Lacy, pulls a left-behind quarter of cigarette from the ashtray nearest her, and lights it.

Bill, the counterman, comes over with Lacy and Franco's orders.

"Damn dirt bag. I make her show her money up front so I don't get stiffed, but she's got the price of toast so what can I do?"

Bill has worked his way in from the periphery where the old lady lives. He still has a penchant for bar fights and a long thin scar along the line of his jaw, as though someone once tried to open his face like an envelope. But he has held down this job for nearly two years and is contemptuous of the panhandlers who winter on Duval Street.

"Now she'll go in the john and puke all over everything because she stuffed herself here after not eating for three days."

"She's still a child of God," Franco says.

17

"Yeah, well, I wish he'd come by and pick her up."

Franco crosses himself to begin a silent prayer for God's forgiveness of Bill's sacrilege. Franco's God is always paying attention. When Franco comes across someone fooling around with what might or might not be amusing to the Almighty, he worries.

Of course, he defines his own terms. What Bill has just said is blasphemy. When Franco, on the other hand, slits the side of his thumb to drop blood on a Big Mac, which he is consecrating as communion at a mass for which the choir is the B-52's on the tape deck, pumping out hip hosannas, this is "personalized liturgy."

He's been escalating some lately. He's taken to wearing formal vestments around town. Lacy says nothing, thinking love has to at least mean allowance.

At the age of forty-two, their Aunt Helen took up where Lacy and Franco's parents abruptly left off. A year earlier she had married for the first time. The groom, Marc Morgan, was much younger. He had been the instructor in Helen's dancercise class. He wore pants tight at the thigh and satin shirts and narrow leather ties. He went to an Oak Street hair stylist who gave him blond highlights. He applied self-tanning gel during months with an *r* in them and sprayed his mouth with little zips of Binaca from a pocket atomizer.

As it turned out, none of this signified. Instead of sliding into the lying about, credit-card abuse, and extracurricular sex anyone would expect, Marc left Vic Tanny's and devoted himself to Helen and the development of her money.

Helen was not a woman with particularly high expectations. She didn't rumple herself wondering if Marc's interest in her was a function of interest in her money. In fact, he turned out to be quite clever with it, slipping into one faddish and extremely risky venture after another, then slipping out with a neat profit just before the particular market saturated or the appeal of the notion collapsed.

Most of the products he backed were advertised in the TV spots just before the national anthem sign-off or in the back pages of supermarket tabloids, just beyond the ads for personalized horoscopes. Marc's products were sold by the pull of mystery and the push of hysteria. Some were connected with weight loss—for instance, Sauna Pants. ("Cannot be bought in stores! Cannot be shown on television! Lose a pound an hour!") Others were gadgets or solvents or foams pitched with great drama for use in the high adventure of housewifery. In this line was Scumaway. ("Problem bath? Get rid of years of grime, slime, lime deposits, soap plaque, rust rings, grout fur. Industrial mask and gloves provided.")

Once in a while Marc would make a fast foray into kitchen aids. As with Omletto, a toaster-sized appliance that accepted two eggs broken into the top and, a few minutes later, ejected a half-moon shaped omelette from a slot in the bottom. ("Brush your teeth and breakfast's ready!")

Until her marriage, Helen had lived on the dividends of sensible investments, so it was surprising that she came to enjoy her new circumstances. Maybe the fact that it all happened so fast—the arrivals of husband and money and nearly grown children in such rapid succession, like so many characters into the Marx Brothers' stateroom—allowed her to take these current events in her life lightly.

A tall, big-boned woman who wore her hair caught up in the back with a small arrangement of tortoise-shell combs, she spent her time performing good works, stimulating herself with culture. Marc Morgan effected a profound change in her. Nothing outwardly obvious; she didn't pull out the combs and let her hair loose and start laughing throaty little laughs. It was more as though Marc entered her in some pervasive way, aerating her, making her a lighter version of herself.

Lacy watched carefully to see if there was something she could pick up that would apply, spreading out the mail-order footprint sheets to see if she might be able to learn the tango.

She was unable to imagine ever letting anyone perform this sort of major molecular rearrangement on her.

Helen's stance toward Lacy and Franco was well off the maternal center. She told them straight away, "It would just be arch for any of us to pretend I'm your mother. If you have something really difficult—if, say, your bedroom is on fire— of course I hope you'll feel free to come to me. I'd be pleased to offer the benefit of what experience I have. But for smaller items, I think you'd just better make your own decisions. What I'm saying is that I'd rather not have to deal with missing socks."

Once in a while Marc would take up the slack, focusing on Lacy and Franco in an attempt to adjust some aspect of their adolescent lives he felt was out of whack. He had a few notions of what normal teenagers should be like. Neither of them fit the bill at all.

He thought they both spent way too much time in the house. Watching movies on the high-number TV channels late into the night, listening to the police call band on their shortwave radio. Reading comics. Playing records from the underside of rock and roll. Smoking up in their rooms. And, of course, the matter of Franco's religious activities.

So Marc went to a wilderness outfitter and bought them a tent, knapsacks, canteens. The idea was to introduce some sunlight and scoutish wholesomeness into their nightshade existence. Marc himself had spent three years in Boy Scouts, accumulating twenty-seven merit badges.

Lacy wasn't interested in anything that could be found in the woods, and Franco was afraid of what might be lurking out there. They didn't want to seem unappreciative, though, and so they got a survival manual and read up on handling rattler bites, escaping quicksand, identifying lethal plants, sending reflector signals to rescue aircraft.

The next morning they set out into the backyard and pitched the tent.

When Marc came out in the afternoon, lifted the flap, and peered into the stale darkness to see them French-inhaling Pall Malls and reading the *Enquirer* and listening to "Louie Louie" on the radio, he dropped the flap and went back up to the house.

"What did he expect?" Franco said.

"I think he hoped we'd have strangled a coyote by now. Roasted it on a spit and made a parka out of its fur. We probably should've gathered something too. Brambles."

"I think brambles are what's between the stuff you gather. I don't think they're ever *what* you're supposed to gather. It's probably in the manual."

"He just wants us to be regular," Lacy said. "He wants you in Little League. He'd like me to be on the phone more."

Franco wasn't listening. After a long time of lying on his back with his eyes closed, his hands clasped behind his head, he said, "Did you ever notice how many similarities there are between the names Franco and Jesus?"

The two of them had by then formed a version of childhood too idiosyncratic to be imposed on by good intentions from the adult world. Their iconoclasm had started much earlier, while their parents were still alive.

Lacy spent about six months of her puberty practicing to be a ventriloquist. She stood every morning in front of the bathroom mirror, talking without moving her lips, working a lot on her b's.

Her hope was to get on a local TV show called *Stairway to the Stars,* which featured kids with talents. Singing sisters. Tap dancing girls in sequined bathing suits. Boy magicians. Girl ventriloquists.

Franco thought the show was hilarious. From the first act, he was gone. He'd start crumpling into weak, weepy laughter, then cover his mouth with both hands and shake. Then lie on the sofa and put a pillow over his head. Lacy ignored him.

Franco was not, to her mind, a reliable authority on entertainment. His favorite show was *Mass for Shut-Ins*. He'd written to NBC with an idea for a *Celebrity Mass for Shut-Ins*.

Lacy's fascination with *Stairway to the Stars* was based in the belief that kids who made it onto the show really were on the first step to stardom, and she saw stardom as a surefire agent for change. If she was a child star, people would be brought in to take care of her—to run her bubble baths, cook her star diet, drive her to the studio. Sensible employees supervised by a studio exec, who would drop in often. Things around her house would get shaped up, just kind of naturally, in the process.

All she needed to get on that first step was a talent. She couldn't sing, never had any tap lessons, had only one untrainable dog. So she asked for a dummy for her birthday. Her parents, not understanding the scope of her ambitions, came up with a disappointing toylike model with one crummy pullstring in the back of its neck to move the jaw up and down. It was a girl doll with red hair named Hildegarde.

In the box was a book, *1001 Two-Part Jokes for All Occasions*. Once Lacy ruled out dialect jokes as too tricky and golf jokes as too specialized, there were really fewer than 1001, but this still left plenty. She built up a routine of a dozen or so. When she had them down pat and had worked up a raspy little voice (incredibly cute, she thought) for Hildegarde, she felt ready to try out the act on her family. As a dry run for the *Stairway*.

She asked everyone to be in the living room that night at eight. Franco refused; he thought the idea of going on a television talent show, particularly with a stupid toy dummy and jokes from a book, was just too pathetic and embarrassing. Lacy didn't take this terribly to heart. He was going through a phase where everything about everybody embarrassed him.

Her parents thought the idea was adorable. They were waiting in the living room when Lacy came down at eight.

Mr. Fitzhugh was there too. Mr. Fitzhugh had been in the lounge at Tom Blackwood's country club three days earlier, had been invited back for a nightcap, and was still there. There were often Mr. Fitzhughs around the house—people who stayed too long to be guests, contributed too little to the household to be considered boarders, were too unrelated to anything going on to be subsumed as extended family.

Lacy's timing was off before she even began. Eight was way too late, way too far into the drinking day of her audience. Her parents and Mr. Fitzhugh had been having pre-show cocktails for two or three hours by then. Things went rather quickly and irretrievably out of kilter. By Lacy's third punchline, her parents' eyes were running with tears and Mr. Fitzhugh had actually tumbled from his chair onto the floor, where he remained, shaking with laughter. Lacy knew these laughs were not "with" her, so to speak. She sunk on the sofa in defeat.

This didn't slow them down. Her father whisked Hildegarde off Lacy's lap and lurched the dummy across the room in a passionate tango. Mr. Fitzhugh got up off the floor and mixed Hildegarde a gimlet. Lacy's mother took Mr. Fitzhugh onto her lap and improvised an act of her own, asking him why the chicken crossed the road. Mr. Fitzhugh replied that it was to keep his pants up.

It was at about this point that Lacy went upstairs.

Her father came to find her the next morning. She was on the sofa in the library, reading a Nancy Drew. She looked up when he came in the room. She felt a hundred years older than he was.

He came over and sat down on the floor in front of her, took her hand and kissed it.

"Sorry," he said.

Lacy stared at the cover of the Nancy Drew. Nancy was hiding beneath a staircase, holding a flashlight.

"We do love you," Tom Blackwood said. "It's just that we don't seem to be much good at this."

This was the year before the roller coaster. The accident horrified but didn't surprise Lacy. Even in life, her parents had been so elusive, so hard to hold by the hand, so quick to disappear around corners. She had lost them hundreds of times before they went out on the coaster. And so she was sort of in practice when it finally happened. Happened finally.

Which should have helped, but didn't. She was more frightened without them than she had been with them. At least while they lived, her fears were specific, close to home. Now she didn't know where the bad news would be lurking.

And Franco was left worse off still. By then they were living in Lake Forest with their Aunt Helen. Lacy tried to help. She took Franco to Riverview, a terrible error in judgment, as it turned out. He wouldn't set foot on any of the rides, not even a wimpy merry-go-round with miniature Jeeps and fire trucks bolted to a revolving floor.

Finally she bought herself a single ticket, not for the roller coaster or the wild mouse or the salt and pepper shakers, just for the Tilt-A-Whirl. She sat alone in her capsule, tilting and whirling, wheee!-ing with ersatz enthusiasm, shaking her hands in the air like pompons, pointing at herself to show how much fun she was having. Then she looked down and saw him, gripping the guard rail with one hand, an uneaten puff of cotton candy with the other. Looking up at her with eyes sick with panicky fear. After that she didn't push him again, even when his fears started winning.

He stopped reading *Tales From the Crypt* and the other ghoulish comics they had both loved, switching to *Archie & Veronica* and *Uncle Scrooge*. Though he would still tag along with her to horror movies, he would leap out to the lobby as soon as the setup was over—as soon as the salesman's car had broken down in the heavy storm on the deserted road by the old house. As soon as the wrong lab beaker had been poured into the tarantulas' food. But even in the lobby he became agitated. Just the sounds of the creature emerging from the lagoon, the mummy creaking out of its coffin, The Slime ooz-ing over Tokyo, were enough to produce bad dreams that brought him into Lacy's room to camp out on the floor next to her bed. From there he moved into being afraid of even non-monster-filled dark. Or perhaps all his darkness was filled with monsters by this time.

After high school he took up languages, but not in the places where they were spoken. Taking the old servant's apart-ment above the garage, he stayed on with Helen and Marc. He took classes at Northwestern and the University of Chicago and wrote Lacy a lot of letters.

She was in Providence then, at art school, going about her life and pretending Franco was going about his in some loose kind of parallel. But she knew all along that what he wanted was convergence with her and that a lot of what he was doing back in Lake Forest was waiting.

At first, to get back at him for this tacit demand, she was cruel by omission. For long stretches she wouldn't write or call; once she moved without sending him a change of address. He responded by simply continuing to wait. Out of school and a collapsed marriage, she stayed in Providence, doing a post-grad-uate year in Uncertainty. She was painting with little confi-dence, waitressing, smoking dope, reading the Tarot in search of next moves. Then one morning, as she was walking down a side street in a light drizzle with a damp sack of groceries, not even thinking about Franco, the power of his longing won out.

It took her only three days to fold her life into her red Camaro convertible and head south. For company she took her bird, a mute parakeet she'd gotten half-price at Wool-worth's. It chirped the first note of its life just after she'd stopped to put the top down, just before they crossed the Georgia–Florida line. She took this as a good omen, though already a lot of the mistakes of her life had been made on the basis of what she took as good omens.

When she hit Key West, there were fifteen years between her and the island. Speeding across the last of the bridges, curving into a sky red with dying sun, she flushed with the pleasure of coming back to some place she'd never been before. She was Magellan with a map.

When she arrived, she found the cabanas were gone from the Casa Marina beach, and no one drank gimlets anymore. Still, the adults awaiting her here, as she came into her own adulthood, were not unlike her parents.

This was mostly a function of geography. Being a southernmost point, the island was an end of the line for those on the run from disappointment—their own or that of sullen wives, armed husbands, rejected paramours, disapproving parents, shadowy debtors. A lot of the people down here, if they'd been doing all right wherever they came from, would still be there.

Key West fulfilled none of their dreams, except maybe small dreamettes of good tips, fishing, or weather. They didn't stay because they were happy, only because there was no farther to go. And they never really left their trouble behind, only replicated it here, against blue-sea–blue-sky horizons, under ceiling fans. Still, Lacy was ecstatic to be back. The past few years of trying to be regular in the regular world had worn her out. It was a relief to get back down here, where oddness was generally viewed as having a point.

With the money she made from selling the house in Lake Forest, she reopened the old one in Key West. She had some roof knocked out for light to paint by, most of the interior walls torn down so they could each have a floor of essentially open space. Then she called Franco and told him everything was ready.

The morning after he arrived, she woke up and went barefoot into the kitchen. Standing at the counter waiting for the Mr. Coffee to start coughing wetly, she looked through the screen, down into the backyard, and saw him. He was sitting amid the overgrown grass and hibiscus in a rusty lawn chair in jeans and a chasuble, his pale thin arms exposed. The vestment was rose-colored, which meant he had just celebrated a mass of rejoicing. He lifted his face toward her, throwing flashes of light her way from his reflector shades.

"Do you think we could make a run out to McDonald's?" he said. "I mean, doesn't it seem like a cheeseburger day?"

Lacy is a finalist for an arts grant—five thousand dollars—given by a small family foundation in Miami. The last stage of the competition is an interview with the foundation's board, at two this afternoon.

She's dreading this. They already like her paintings; why do they also have to like her? She feels like the Miss America contestant who is already blonde and from Mississippi but is still being required to perform on the zither and have a plan for world peace. Lacy sulks as she showers. She puts on a plain black cotton dress she hopes will be pleasing to the elderly, since she assumes the foundation people will be old.

In the bucket seat next to her, Franco sits rigid and silent. She's dropping him at the dentist while she goes for the interview. She found this place for him in Miami Beach, a hip dental clinic that caters to people who think dentists are Nazis.

"Hello, Francis," says the dulcet-toned receptionist, blending in with the Windam Hillish number on the sound system. "Have a seat why don't you?" She gestures to a small grouping of gray recliners. The room is painted a soft peach and has low, indirect lighting. Lacy, having been here barely thirty seconds, is already feeling like taking a nap.

"I'll be back in an hour," she tells Franco, but he's already locked into a clench, sitting rigid on the edge of a recliner.

"Honey," she says. He doesn't hear her. Just as she's beginning to feel inadequate to the situation, there's a soft hand on her shoulder. She turns and looks up. It's the receptionist. Lacy stands.

"We'll be giving Francis his relaxant in just a moment," she reminds Lacy. This is euphemistic for the ten-milligram Valium all Tooth Shop patients receive to ease their way toward the chair.

"Ah," Lacy says and looks back at Franco. It doesn't seem like mere Valium will be able to put a significant dent in his anxiety. He already looks as though he's being mildly electrocuted, and he's only here today for a cleaning. She doesn't know what she'll do if she ever has to bring him in for a filling or, heaven forbid, root canal work. "Maybe..." she starts to say, but then sees that she is being ushered out, the receptionist's hand expertly pocketing her elbow.

"It's sometimes better if the patient's support mechanisms are transferred to our Total Care System."

Lacy nods as though leaving is her idea, as though she's not being thrown out.

When she comes out of the clinic, she is immediately drenched in sweat. The day is ferociously hot. She tries to hold her arms out from her sides a little as she drives, so she won't walk into the interview with huge wet stains at the pits of her dress. She imagines a Clown Foundation. The CF would require no forms in quadruplicate, no slides, no interviews. You just get a call to come to their tent. Inside, three clowns sit, each behind a big barrel of money. As soon as you walk in, they chuckle and wiggle their fingers at you and say, "Now don't tell us what you want this money for. Just tell us how much."

And when you name an absolutely outrageous figure, they say, "Oh that can't be enough. Here. Take more."

And they run out from behind their barrels and grab handfuls of large-denomination bills and stuff your pockets and then honk the horns on their belts and bop each other on the head with foamy mallets and squirt each other (but not you) with seltzer bottles, and then usher you out with jostling shoves and bursts of tickling.

There are no clowns at the French Foundation. The offices are on the top floor of a high-rise overlooking Biscayne Bay. They are painted blue and white and have a celestial atmosphere, as if what goes on here is the answering of prayers rather than just the dispensing of money.

There are only two people. One if them is Violet French, who is the oldest person Lacy has ever seen. Lacy needn't have worn the plain dress for her, though. She is another, more Floridian variant of old, someone who is clearly giving Death the raspberry, refusing to go quietly. Mummified with tan and swathed in brilliantly-colored scarves, she smells like chlorine—a smell Lacy, a swimmer herself, can identify at fifty paces. Violet French is doing such a good job of holding off the inevitable, looks so good for her age, that Lacy knows she must be even older than she looks, and she looks to be about a hundred.

She has a few questions for Lacy. They're whimsical, not written down, and don't seem to be in any particular direction. Does Lacy think there's a mystical element to her work?

She supposes so.

Has she ever experimented with nutritional control in connection with her painting?

Lacy's not sure what this question means but begins to see that her role in this situation is that of small juicy mouse being play-mauled a little by an old cat. Sitting next to Mrs. French and enjoying her questions is her grandson Russell.

He's about Lacy's age. He slouches, grins with his eyes, and wears stylishly wrinkled clothes. Lacy doesn't return his little eye-smiles, and she doesn't answer his grandmother's questions very interestingly, either. She's through with bothering to be any good at this.

"Do you agree that art reached its highest peak during the epochs of royal patronage?" Violet French asks now, but Lacy can tell her heart's gone out of this, because Lacy is not being nearly enough fun. When the phone rings, Mrs. French takes the call without excusing herself, one-handedly gathering up the papers and plastic sheets of Lacy's slides and passing them over to Russell.

Who accompanies Lacy out. They stand silently within the equally silent elevator. He stands slightly behind Lacy. She can't even hear him breathe, but his presence is aggressive at her back. When the car stops and the brushed chrome doors part, he moves too quickly and bumps into her on their way out. At first Lacy takes this as an accident, but then Russell gives himself away with a fillip, a small, almost imperceptible, rubbing move of his groin against some unspecified erogenous zone, somewhere between Lacy's hip and her ass.

When they reach the revolving door, she turns and shakes his hand briskly and walks across the asphalt—so hot at this hour that the tar patches are bubbling up—and gets into the Camaro. She has forgotten, of course, to put the top up or spread a towel on the seat, and so has to pretend she is not getting third-degree burns on the back of her calves as she starts the car. And floods it. He stands watching her for a minute while she sits waiting for the gas line to clear; then he starts coming toward her. He has wide hips and a wide face and is now slipping on small horn-rim sunglasses that are the height of fashion, but wrong for him. They make him look even more panda-like. She waves him off.

"It's okay," she shouts lightly. "I just have to wait until it's ready."

He keeps coming. When he gets there, he puts his hands on the chrome door trim and has to pretend he's not getting third-degree burns on his palms.

"We'll be giving your application careful attention," he says. Shielding her eyes against the sun, Lacy can no longer see his head. She looks into an expanse of wrinkled pink oxford cloth and crumpled green rep tie. "I should say it looks good. It could be looking very good. If we could, maybe, talk a little more. Perhaps in a less formal setting..."

She thinks for a second or two about the five grand and decides it's a fair price for getting to put the Camaro into gear and drive off on Russell French in mid-sentence.

Franco is in the waiting room at The Tooth Shop when she gets there. He's all the way back in one of the recliners. She takes the one next to him and pushes it back and sighs as her body takes a huge hit off the Shop's state-of-the-art air-conditioning.

"It was so stupid," she tells him.

He doesn't say anything.

"If I were any kind of real artist, I'd get interviews with real foundations, not dating services rich old ladies set up for their little boys."

When Franco still doesn't respond, Lacy realizes she is nattering on to someone who has been smoothed out with Valium and numbed with novocaine and sitting for an hour inside headphones pumping out New Age tones. When he finally turns to look at her, he stretches his mouth into a wide fake smile and taps a tooth with a fingernail.

L acy has been working through the afternoon. The heavy fronds of the coconut palm outside the window brush the screen next to her so roughly it sounds like rain. The elements tend to blur down here. The surf at a distance approximates wind. The sky at sunset is fire.

Franco comes in the door at the far end of the studio.

"The little red light's on here, on your message machine," he says. "Let's see who called you." He rewinds the tape, puts it on playback, and falls onto the yellow couch. He loves this machine, but doesn't have one of his own. Doesn't have a phone. Lacy picks up what few messages come in for him. Ostensibly this is why he wants to listen to the tape, but it's really to nose around in her business. It's rolling now.

"*This is Optix. Your sunglasses are ready. You can pick them up any time.*" Long pause. "*Goodbye.*"

"*Harry here. Any more Noirs you want to part with? I have someone interested. Let me...*" It cuts off there.

"Oh, good," Lacy says. "I've those three left. If he can sell them, we have the next couple of months covered."

The tape is still rolling. Jack's voice comes on.

*"I'm making fish stew this afternoon. It should be ready around seven."*

"Boy does he work at it," Franco says. "Have you ever heard anyone sound so smooth just talking to a tape? He sounds like he's talking to a person. And not just a person on the other end of the line. More like a person wearing his pajama top."

"Come here," Lacy says. "I've something I want you to see." She gestures toward the canvas on her easel. He gets up and comes around.

"It's nearly done," she says. *Marilyn Monroe Sings 'Happy Birthday' to JFK.*

"It's great," he says, but doesn't mean it. Franco doesn't think much of this stuff. He thinks Lacy ought to be taking more chances. He tells her it's okay with him if they starve, but she knows he's thinking of romantic starvation, not the real thing.

"I've got only one more to go after this," she says, waving her hand around the studio where the rest of these paintings are propped against walls on window sills. "The other half of the pair, *Jackie O. Pensive on Skorpios.*"

"They'll be a big hit," he says, looking out the window "Especially down here. Blow that driftwood right out of the shop."

A dolescence came out pretty much of a wash for Lacy. She couldn't figure out the bases on which popularity was granted, couldn't keep up the required attention to detail—shades of cordovan, tininess of flowers in paisley prints, relative rankings of country club memberships.

She went through four years at the same level of loneliness. In a time when other girls were having their hair cut short and shaped, frosting the front, she wore hers long and heavy. In a fluffed-up, bouffant era, she was tall and skinny, brooding and overearnest. Flat-chested and hipless in a season of curves and breasts. On the swim team when being a girl jock was only slightly higher on the social scale than being in the really embarrassing clubs—Future Nuns and Sacristeens. Plus she spent her weekends painting. Everyone found this very queer. She wasn't much interested in the available pool of boys. Queerer still.

She still couldn't bring other kids home. Although Helen was impeccably presentable, Marc passably so, they were distracted by each other and hadn't noticed Franco progressing further and further into the religiously lurid. Clouds of incense often hung in the upstairs hallway. Holy pictures would suddenly turn up magneted to the refrigerator door. Not the usual Midwest whitebread pictures of Jesus looking like James Garner with a neatly trimmed beard. She figured Franco must have had to send off to Bogotá or Palermo for his stuff. Obscure devotional madonnas with rhinestoned eyelids and toenails. Embalmed saints in glass caskets. Graphic depictions of out-of-the-way martyrdoms. He was also fascinated with the notion of apparitions, collected historical accounts of church-recognized phenomena. Tabloid accounts too—the housewife from New Jersey who claimed she saw the face of Jesus in her screen door, the girl from Managua who said Saint Rose spoke to her over the radio. He confided to Lacy that he was experiencing apparitions himself, that sometimes in the middle of one of his evening devotions to the Sacred Heart, Christ in the picture would tap his exposed heart and then point at Franco.

"It's just something he does," Franco said by way of explanation.

When she applied to schools, she skipped Chicago's Art Institute, even though they had a strong painting program. She needed to cut loose for a while. From Franco, and from the whole loony past of her family. She was relieved when an acceptance arrived from the Rhode Island School of Design, and set off for Providence full of the spirit of being On Her Own.

She got the last room in a high frame house on Lloyd Street. The room was twenty feet by six. Someone immediately gave her an old set of bowling pins to set at one end.

There were four other rooms on the floor plus a communal bath. The girls who lived in these rooms cooked canned macaroni and cheese on the hotplate in the bathroom, made instant coffee with an electric coil, drank Tabs that were only ever as cold as it was on the window sill. They talked about

Camus and Orwell, Braque, O'Keeffe, Wee Gee, the Stones. Two were lit majors at Pembroke. The other three were art students.

One, like Lacy, was majoring in painting. She aspired to be a muralist and had her walls tacked with graph paper block-outs for the *Great Scenes From Literature,* a project she'd been commissioned to do on the brick wall of a branch of the public library, facing a parking lot shared with a veterinarian's office. It was a start. She was optimistic about getting a hearty reception from a world that just hadn't heard of her yet. Her name was Pam Fields. She turned out to be Lacy's first great friend, the donor of the bowling pins, and briefly, Lacy's first lover.

Their falling in love happened quite rapidly. It was identifying the emotion, acknowledging it, and expressing it that took nearly a year to sort out. Months during which their into-the-night discussions shifted from everything but them to them. A time during which little presents to each other went from sketch books to slender volumes of romantic verse from the women's bookstore to small battered lockets and rings from junk shops. It was all the way to the end of spring term, all the way to dawn of their longest night of talking before they finally slipped into Pam's bed, making up the rest as they went along. From there everything went very fast— mutual and instant decisions to stay for summer term, which left them alone in the house, free to fall openly into each other while at the same time staying safely hidden.

These three months were the first time in Lacy's life that she'd felt really free. She put her worries about Franco on hold, even in the face of a letter from Helen, who was a little unsettled by the regular Saturday-afternoon arrival from who knows where of two old women in babushkas who were apparently coming to her brother for confession. Lacy didn't feel any of the usual pressure to make something of herself. There were few courses offered in the summer term. She and Pam took the same morning life-drawing studio and then a twentieth-century photo-history survey, which let them out by noon. They usually had lunch in a remote corner of Prospect Park, dinner at one of the cheap Italian restaurants on the hill. In between they climbed up onto a small, obscured patch of flat roof above the back stairs of their house, peeled off their jeans and T-shirts, and made out under deep-blue skies. Lacy felt that all of her life until this had just been a foyer.

Then fall arrived. Lacy thought they should face the real world head-on and just move into the attic double together, tacitly announcing their relationship, letting people take it as they would. Pam had another approach to the problem. She moved into an apartment closer to campus and announced her engagement to a guy named Skipper, a Tri Delt she'd dated the year before and had made fun of to Lacy for his adenoidal voice and pipe-smoking affectations.

Lacy tried calling and got brushed off or worse—got Skipper. Then she moved on to writing fourteen-draft letters, all of which went unanswered. She spent her entire sophomore year in a state of fluish heartbreak. If she either breathed in too fast or thought too directly about Pam Fields, she'd get a sharp pain just beneath her breastbone. At some point, way into this, she wore herself out, and decided to (a) just fucking move on and (b) never feel this bad again.

She began to try boys—other art students who gathered up their courage with long discussions of post-painterly abstraction before unzipping their fatigues and making the lunge. Although there was a certain blunt urgency to these connections, they were ultimately too tied up with wines from surprising countries drunk out of goatskins and last-minute foldings-out of sofas and frantic morning-after hopes pinned on the spermicidal properties of raspberry douche to qualify as thrilling. But they gave her a body of experience from which to infer. Because she felt so much with Pam, so little in these subsequent involvements, she concluded that she had slid irretrievably into cynicism.

She started hanging out with a fringe group of guys who were making their collective artistic statement by taking no classes and making no art. TJ was just one of these guys. There wasn't much about him that set him off from the others. He was the less pudgy of the two pudgy ones, the most articulate of the three or four quiet ones. He had the most advanced receding hairline.

When she met him, he was living in a basement apartment tricked out with blue lights. He spent most of his time in bed, listening to tapes of recorder music, and growing his nails. He'd heard that you could get hundreds of dollars for a full set if they were an inch long. At some point during the first few weeks she knew him—and not through anything so active as a decision—she moved out of the boarding house and in with him. This was the beginning of what would essentially amount to two gentle, goofy months followed by two years of breaking up. The two years' part was mostly pointed silences mixed with oblique dialogue and superficial analyses of their relationship. The set was the basement apartment with its overstuffed, mushroomy-smelling furniture, sound-tracked by a seemingly endless version of "Greensleeves." At some nearly random point in this conversation, they got married.

Lacy hadn't intended to marry anyone, ever. But there came a moment when TJ was feeling especially low, and he thought a little ceremony might cheer him up. It seemed churlish to deny him something that had so little importance to her, and so they went down to City Hall the day their blood passed muster. The judge was a middle-aged woman. She was reading the paper when they came in, and didn't acknowledge their presence until she finished her article, folded the paper, and put it aside. Then she took off her glasses and said, "All rise."

Lacy and TJ stepped up to the bench. The judge wound up and flicked on a small music box that sat between them and her and played "Love Theme From Romeo and Juliet" through the three minutes of their ceremony. The kitsch was lost on TJ, who had eaten some peyote buttons beforehand and afterward told everyone that they had been married "inside a musical rainbow."

Getting married cheered him up only for a very short while. Then he went back to being depressed, and from there to being angry with Lacy. The anger took the shape of tossed stereo components and pages ripped out of Lacy's art books, and a morning when she woke to find him way too awake on his side of the bed.

"I was just lying here," he said, "thinking about nicking little slices out of your legs with an exacto knife."

The ostensible reason for his anger was her betrayal. She had dropped out of his nihilistic circle, and dropped back into school within a term, responding to a telegram from Marc after he'd seen her grades—all withdrawals. The telegram read, "Off your duff or come back home." By the time she was in her senior year, she was on the honors list, getting paintings shown in the student gallery. But this wasn't the real rub between them. TJ himself painted on the sly—Kmart Pollacks that came out of orgies of tossing acrylics against draped tarps. On summer weekends, he took them down to Boston and sold them at art fairs.

The real problem between them was the mutual embarrassment of discrepancy. They both knew that Lacy would never feel anything about TJ that would bring her to book ripping or leg nicking. She would never put snakes in his sock drawer for spite or menstrual blood in his food to keep him faithful. She'd never ask the Ouija board if he was in her future or write his name in her notebook and outline all the letters. The fact was, she sometimes forgot what he took in his coffee, and she could never remember the color of his eyes.

And so it was more out of fair play than fear that Lacy got a Man With Van out of the phone book and over to her house one morning as soon as TJ had left for coffee with the guys at the Union. In the years that followed, she almost forgot she'd ever been married to him until a day when a guy in a Searsy suit showed up one day at her door with divorce papers.

L acy messes up on the last details on the last of the "Modern Myths" canvases. This often happens, a balking at the finish line. The best place for her is having it knocked without having it done. Once it's really done, it's up for criticism, dead behind her with something completely unbegun lying ahead. She's been in this spot before. It's nothing serious. She can give herself over to it, just take a break. She decides to drive up to Sugarloaf Key, pay Jack a little visit.

She changes into shorts and a T-shirt, throws some high-gear paraphernalia into the car. A billed fisherman's cap to keep her hair out of her face crossing the wind-whipped bridges. A can of red pop. Her boom box. The Camaro only has AM and she likes to keep the hits coming. This takes quick switching coming up through the Keys, where you can pull in only a couple of stations at a time, hold on to them for only a couple of songs.

At Sugarloaf she takes the turnoff to Jack's house. It's a huge dilapidated place, set above a small cove. She figures he'll be in his studio and so takes the sandy path that leads around back. He's there in the garden between the house and the studio. It's an overgrown plot with long grass tangled up in itself. The borders are gardenia bushes. The scent is overwhelming, like the powder room of an old movie theater after someone has pressed every button on the perfume dispenser machine.

He doesn't hear her come up behind him. He's kneeling, cutting huge white flowers from one of the bushes pressing against a low side fence. The fence is wood and sea-beaten and ferociously shedding its remaining paint in large flakes.

"Hey," she says softly, trying not to startle him.

He turns and smiles and stands, flowers in one hand, clippers dangling from the other, smears of sandy earth across the knees of his shapeless khakis. He moves as though the various parts of his body are only loosely connected. He looks at her for a moment without saying anything. The only sound between them is the hissing of an unseen lawn sprinkler.

"Atmosphere," he says, holding up the gardenias. "I'm painting a lady from Islamorada. She's wearing white linen, and I'm surrounding her with white flowers. She's had four husbands, but would like the painting to give her a 'virginal look.' We aim to please."

Jack can't afford too much irony in his line of work. Less than Lacy even. He does portraits with swirling pastel backgrounds setting off subjects who hail from the periphery of the upper class. The paintings feature women seated in wicker chairs. Fathers and children in matching polo shirts. All of them bathed in a liquidy light that insinuates itself from one direction, as if the setting is a sun room or terrace. As if the subject has been snatched for a moment from a life spent on the lope, in civilized portions of the out-of-doors. Courts and courses.

Jack's subjects are brought in from how they actually look to some more central point of attractiveness. He shortens noses and lengthens necks and adds intelligence behind eyes, but only by the smallest increments, so that the viewer will think not that the likeness is flattering but that his estimation of the subject has not, until now, been high enough. It's a ne.. trick and one that makes Jack popular among local gentry who can afford this sort of document.

Now he stands massaging the back of his neck with the knuckles of the hand holding the gardenias, smoothing out a minor problem.

"What are you doing here?" he says.

"You said you were making spaghetti."

"That was two days ago, and it was fish stew. I can't do anything about you right now. The lady from Islamorada is due."

"You're pissed off."

"No. I'm happy to see you. But I'm too old for caprice."

She and Jack have been off and on with each other for a couple of years.

She drives back and he shows up later, around eight, starving. They go over to the raw bar. He eats like an Italian stockbroker, elegantly ravenous. He inhales steam off the conch chowder as if it's vapor from an elixir. He stirs the soup slowly, looks into it as if expecting to find meaning rather than potatoes and carrots. He eats it in alternation with ripped-off hunks of bread and long drinks of draft beer from an iced mug.

From there he moves on to the stone crab, where he's in charge with pick and cracker. Lacy enjoys watching him. Earlier at home she microwaved an off-brand frozen Egg McMuffin. It strikes her that more and more of what she eats is food that has been broken down, reformed in parody of itself, suspended by freezing, rejuvenated by waves, all in imitation of the imitation food served in franchise restaurants.

"I think I have a suitor," she tells Jack. "That guy from the foundation in Miami. He's been steaming up my phone machine." This is really stretching it. Russell French actually called only once, to get an address to send her slides back. She can't remember having tried before to make Jack jealous. She's not doing it now to any particular purpose. It's just something to do.

"Oh," Jack says, wringing his hands and screwing his face into a stage wince. "I do hope he's not more handsome than I am. Or younger. Does he drive a Jag sedan? That would really kill me." He won't be any fun at all in this.

"How can you be so sure of me?" she says. "Don't you even have the odd fleeting doubt?"

He pauses for a minute.

"I think what I am is the opposite of being sure of you. I don't think I've ever had you at all. You're with me for lack of a better offer. Someday you'll run into someone you want much more than you want me. Probably someone really terrible. And then you'll bolt, and that'll be that. All of a sudden. Like a heart attack. No way to worry about it in advance. And until it happens, I've got you. You're not going to go for this foundation guy. You know he'll have one of those trays on his dresser—for his change and cuff links. He'll wear cuff links. You'll have to go up to his apartment and watch him smell the cork from the wine and put the Pachelbel Canon on the stereo like it's a discovery. And then you'll have to pretend to be seduced. Really. You don't have the patience for that sort of stuff anymore. You like your connections direct, and I'm your man there."

"Does that mean you'll go out to the car with me now?" she says.

"I think, here in the real world, we have to pay up first."

"No. We can come back for coffee. We won't be gone long. We won't even be missed."

L acy keeps it simple. Her part of the house is sparsely furnished—the yellow sofa in the studio, an old wooden table and chairs in the kitchen. She has a few glasses and forks and plates. Two frying pans, a large and a small. She buys a day or two worth of groceries at a time. She has enough underwear and jeans to go a couple of weeks between laundry days. She has an extra set of sheets in case she spills some Chinese carry-out in bed. She's wary of the weight of things.

Not Jack. Everything around him is heavy baggage with no porters in sight. His house is in terrible repair, with porch steps that sag like hammocks, roof gutters groaning with wet palm fronds, faucets that drip so badly they hardly need to be turned on to be used. The house is filled with a floating population of ex-wives and grown children, and friends and lovers and spouses and children of these children. With them come trunks and backpacks, looms and harpsichords, video games and cocker spaniels, bicycles and a driveway full of cars.

Overwhelming all this action is the inertly powerful presence of Jack's mother, who is dying in the small front parlor.

This part of the house is saturated with the smells of liniment and boxed chocolates. Anyone coming in the front passes her doorway. Because of the position of the bed, only her feet are visible. Sometimes Lacy can imagine that the pink slippers hold the feet of a napping person, but other times there is a set to them that makes her certain they are awake feet.

No one sees much of her. She doesn't want visitors. She is held in desperate fascination with her pain. In her stillness and silence, though, she inadvertently dominates the house and keeps its population restless and transient. Everyone arrives in the middle of some piece of trouble—emotional, financial—and leaves as soon as the errant lover has come around, the check come through. Jack slumps from the shoulders under the weight of this household.

"The closer I get to you, the more I feel your fatigue," she says to him now. They've just made love and are lying side-by-side, not touching. It's one of those tradewindless summer nights when skin on skin has Velcro aspects and sex is about the only good enough reason to touch someone.

"You don't see that there's also something reassuring about wives and children and mortgage payments and a garage full of useless lawnmowers. When I'm surrounded, it's easy to find my place. You have responsibilities too. Your work, your house, Franco."

"Well, Franco's more like a present."

Jack thinks Lacy ought to be getting Franco to a shrink, that she's caretaking a mental invalid and kidding herself that she's just hanging out with her brother. He also thinks she should not be trusting Harry Windsor as utterly as she does. He thinks she ought to dye her hair red. He loves redheads.

Lacy thinks his children abuse his generosity. She thinks anyone who is fifty-three and smokes and drinks and gets no exercise ought to clean up his act.

They've formed an easy, if superficial, companionship by not wandering too often into these topics.

Jack's room is in the attic of the house. It has three ceiling fans in the rafters and large windows at both ends, and so tonight is unusual—there's usually at least a lapping cross breeze. On stormy nights, it's like a scene from *Jamaica Inn*. His bed has an iron frame and is set at one end of the room, by the windows that overlook the gulf, and so the view from there is all sea.

He's asleep now and Lacy is looking out, watching lanterns on the night-fishing boats, so distant they look like fireflies. She's sitting up against the head of the bed, naked with a large ashtray on her legs, smoking one of his cigarettes. She has no idea how late it is. She looks at him now while his body is vulnerable to inspection. It's a body with some mileage on it. There's a thick heaviness to it that has more to do with age than with weight. His chest has dropped a little and has an indentation at the center, his stomach lies in small folds. She likes his imperfection. It frees her from worrying about her appendectomy scar, the small pot belly she gets before her period, the backs of her calves, which she often misses shaving in the shower. Someone more perfect would have to be lived up to, deserved, might reject her. Jack won't reject her. He thinks he's a lucky guy to have her. She's nearly twenty years younger than he is, is lively company, makes no demands. What Lacy gets in return is a friend she can sleep with without the tenor ever leaping into grand passion. She can feel a lot for Jack, think a lot about him and still get work done, still go about an uninterrupted life. Mostly this seems like a terrific deal. Mostly.

When she finishes the cigarette, the first she's smoked in months, she leaves quietly so as not to wake him. She drives back home. She knows Franco will still be awake, waiting. He has trouble falling asleep when she's still out. She picks up a video at the 7-Eleven. The selection at four a.m. is pretty slim; the best she can come up with is *Blue Hawaii*.

A few nights later Lacy is feeling low and edgy at the same time. She calls Heather and asks if they can meet at Pier House for a drink. On her way out she passes Franco's door. It's Friday and so he's saying the Stations of the Cross. He started this as a simple staged reading, but it has by now gotten pretty Cecil B. DeMille. He takes the part of Christ and plays opposite a large cast of supporting characters—Mary Magdalene, assorted apostles, Roman soldiers, Pontius Pilate. He has all of them recorded on his tape deck. Lacy suspects there are also costumes and props, but doesn't particularly want details.

She pauses at his door, though, and listens for a moment. She hears his cross dragging along the floor. He stops to ask Veronica if he can wipe his face on her veil. A high-pitched Franco on the tape answers, "Sure." Then the live Franco says, "Ronnie, when this is all over, don't forget to send the shroud to Turin."

Franco thinks Jesus was a lot wittier than people think. He's trying to work this into his liturgy.

Heather is already at the bar when Lacy gets there. There aren't too many tourists. The crowd thins way out in summer. The entertainment gets worse too. Tonight there's a female singer so lacking in presence that people aren't taking her as an act. Two couples are dancing around her as though she's a jukebox.

Heather and Lacy find a booth off in the back so they can talk. Heather is a sculptor. She's been going through a rough patch, working for some time now on oversized mud sculptures of easy chairs. Everyone finds these interesting, but so far no one has given her gallery space for them. She's hanging tough, though.

Heather stands out on this island. She's pale and freckled, impervious to tan. She wears Kmart blouses buttoned to the top and thick-lensed glasses. She has red hair that she cuts herself with a Trimcomb. All of this should put her out of the social running, but instead combines like proteins in some way that makes her compelling to an endless stream of beautiful women. Lacy mostly holds her friendship in reserve. She doesn't want to use her up or wear her out. Heather has a lot of liens on her time and energy. Her art, for one thing. She has a daughter. To support both of these, she sells herbal cosmetics and teaches crafts to old people and hawks wind chimes at the sunsets. Also, at the moment, she is consumed by love.

Claudia, the beloved, is Italian. She's a voluptuously tragic figure, enervated by a mysterious and presumably harrowing past. She gives off the air of someone recuperating. She has eyes of a brown so deep that you can't see where the iris stops and the pupil begins. Her hair tumbles. She speaks English with an accent that makes it seem as though everyone else got it all wrong. She dresses in white and makes dinners of spaghetti tossed with the unexpected. Heather says she's heaven in bed. And that she expects to eventually lose her.

"She's working through something. I'm frightened that when she finally gets to the other side, she'll disappear."

Lacy is glad Heather didn't bring Claudia along tonight. This way they can talk. When Claudia is around, there's an erotic gauze that winds itself around all three of them, as though they're on a long, low white sofa in a large, white room opening onto the bay of Naples. Lacy has trouble concentrating. Tonight, though, she can be self-absorbed and complaining.

"I'm all nerved up lately," she says.

"I thought you had everything worked out so you wouldn't ever have to be all nerved up."

"Is that true?" Lacy says, then lets go of her coyness. "It is true. It's true."

"It's not the worst way in the world to operate. Safe setups."

"But..." Lacy says, anticipating.

"Well, it's not foolproof. The only foolproof insurance against nerves is pure fearlessness, and that's hard to come by."

"I don't even know what it is I'm afraid of."

"Oh, you could probably take a guess," Heather says.

She has to pick up her daughter from a dance class. Lacy stays behind for a second glass of wine, then gets up to leave. On her way out she ducks into the ladies' room. It's empty except for an attendant, sitting on a folding campstool by the sinks, holding a stack of torn-off paper towels on her lap. It's the vagrant woman from the other day in Huey's. She looks a little less vagrant tonight. She's wearing what at first appears to be a uniform. On closer inspection, Lacy sees that the white top is a dentist's jacket. DR. MUNOZ is embroidered above the breast pocket. The slacks are pilled brown stretch pants in a fabric that has inherent shimmering properties. She looks up suddenly, catches Lacy's glance, and grins and greets her hugely, as if they share a distant but important piece of past, like rooming together in college.

"Well, well, well," she says.

Lacy goes into one of the stalls. When she comes out, the woman says, "Not bad. Not a bad night at all. I'm nearly up to the price of supper. I enjoy dining late. It's more Continental."

"They don't care when you take off then?" Lacy says.

"Who's *they*?"

"Well, the hotel."

She looks at Lacy as if she has just said, "the interplanetary visitors," but hands her a towel anyway.

"They don't know I'm here. They give me the quick boot if they find me. That's why I have to spread myself around. I come here maybe only once every two weeks, even though it's the best place on the island. The rest of the circuit's not so good for tips. The worst is McDonald's, of course."

This stops Lacy for a second.

"Aren't women surprised to find an attendant in the john at McDonalds?"

"Well, I suppose they might be. But they don't say anything. And they do tip. But *small*. Kiddo, I have gotten *pennies* at McDonald's. Of course, they don't have towels there. All I can do for them is punch the button on the hand blower."

Lacy pulls two quarters out of her pocket and goes to drop them on the saucer. The woman intercepts them with an amazingly fast hand before they land.

"Well," she says, "that's a wrap."

She gets up and is clearly on her way out, which means that they are on their way out together. She stays in step with Lacy through the lobby, out the side door, and into the parking lot.

"Where do you eat?" Lacy says.

"You know the diner over by the Conch Train depot."

"You walk all the way out there?"

"And then back to the shrimp docks. I have a place out there. I live with some other people. We have some boxes."

"How do you mean?" Lacy says.

"Boxes. You know. Refrigerators come in them."

"Aren't there places where you can go?" Lacy says.

"Oh, yes, indeed, there are places. It's the places that make the boxes look good. Although nowadays my box is going bad. After a few good rains, they're never the same. It's not the box it used to be."

They've reached Lacy's car.

"Why don't I give you a lift over?" Lacy hears herself say.

"A car," the woman says, running her hand over the back fender as if it's a horse's flank. "There's nothing like a car, is there?" She opens the door and climbs into the back seat.

Her name is Mrs. Crooks. She doesn't offer a first name. Lacy asks, over her shoulder, how long she's been down here.

"A few weeks. I came after Christmas." It's now June.

"Where're you from?"

"Oh, here and there. I like to keep on the go. Here it is." She thrusts her whole arm out to point. Lacy pulls into the dirt lot in front, shifts into neutral, keeps the motor running.

"You want to come in?" Mrs. Crooks says.

"I'm pretty tired."

"A cup of coffee will pick you right up. I don't get much company. Leastways not the kind anyone'd want."

She turns to find the woman looking at her with more eagerness than can be easily put off. She turns back, shuts the ignition down, and slides the key out.

Lacy has never been here. For a diner, it's dimly lit. A lot of the fluorescents overhead are dead or dying, and so everything is bathed in a nervous, wavering green. There are maybe half a dozen people at the counter and in the booths. They look like they all shot up together in the bathroom five minutes earlier. A cleanup guy is wheeling around a string mop in this month's bucket of ammonia water and sloshing it here and there desultorily. People lift their feet without breaking the momentum of eating or talking as he swipes underneath them. On the jukebox, George Jones is singing "When Your Phone Don't Ring, That's Me." At first Lacy thinks it's some extended-play version, then realizes it's just repeating endlessly. Either the jukebox is broken, or someone is using up a lot of quarters to bleed a mood.

As they wait in their booth, Lacy watches plates go by, topped with amorphous masses of gray, green, and brown. Maximum-security cuisine.

"I'll just have coffee," she tells the waitress, a woman with fat upper arms that make the sleeves of her uniform look like shiny aqua tourniquets. Her legs are spotted with tied-off varicose veins. Lacy wishes she could make her smile. She'd like to buy her a chateau in Switzerland and hire her a naughty chauffeur.

"There's a two-buck minimum in the booths. You'll have to pay it even if you have just the coffee." She sighs and shifts her weight as though Lacy is being difficult and she's just going to have to wait out this little tantrum. Lacy thinks she would be nicer if she knew about the chateau.

"We'll have some blueberry pie," Mrs. Crooks says, giving Lacy a broad stage wink. For herself, she orders the pork chop plate with fries and gravy. The waitress makes no acknowledgment of the order except to leave.

"I'll eat your pie too," Mrs. Crooks says, as if she's doing Lacy a favor.

Lacy makes a few more attempts at eliciting history from her, but Mrs. Crooks wants to stay in the present tense. She has a scheme, to sluice off some of the tourist money floating around in pockets at the sunsets down on Mallory Docks. She is going to bake horoscopes into chocolate chip cookies. She's only lacking an oven.

"So you're a student of astrology," Lacy says.

"Don't be silly," she says and pulls from the doctor's jacket pocket a limp piece of filler paper. She flattens the list out and pushes it across the table.

Lacy reads, STICK BY PHONE. CALL IS COMING. FORGET THE CREEP. SOMEONE BETTER'S AROUND THE CORNER. GO AHEAD AND CHARGE IT. MONEY'S ON WAY.

"I give them what they want to hear."

As Mrs. Crooks speaks, Lacy watches her teeth. They look

like she ordered them by mail. Or picked them out from a selection of seven sizes at Woolworth's dental department. They're too long and too beige, and click when she talks, so that all her words seem as though they are simultaneously being spoken and typed. And she's unstoppable as a charging rhino. She keeps on talking and clicking through dinner, two cups of coffee tricked to the limit with cream and sugar, a sample pack of some new brand of cigarettes. After all this, she stops, belches softly into a small, wadded-up paper napkin, pats her stomach and smiles.

"Always nice to have a chat," she says, although Lacy has barely said anything. Now she does. She says she'd better be going.

"Me too. All of a sudden, I'm bushed," Mrs. Crooks says.

Lacy gets up to get a check, comes back to find Mrs. Crooks lying down, sound asleep on her side of the booth. The waitress, radar-equipped, is immediately on the scene.

"You'll have to roust her out of here pronto. Boss says she's taking no more snoozes on the premises."

Lacy looks down at Mrs. Crooks, who is well beyond napping at this point. She's into REM-3 sleep. Suddenly Lacy is responsible for her. The waitress is standing with arms crossed, actually tapping with one foot like an exasperated cartoon character. Wilma Flintstone miffed at Fred.

Lacy tries leaning over and shaking her by the shoulder, gently. No response. Harder. Still nothing. Harder yet.

There's no picking her up. She outweighs Lacy by fifty pounds. Lacy turns and shrugs. The waitress takes this as license to go into action. She leans past Lacy, picks up a glass of water from the table and pours it dispassionately over Mrs. Crooks's head. Surprisingly, this does not make her start. She lies there a few seconds longer, then reaches up and gropes around on the tabletop until her hand finds a napkin. Sitting up, blotting herself, she smiles at Lacy and the waitress and says, "I'm sorry, but I'm afraid I'll have to be leaving now."

There are several boxes in the far corner of the fields down by the shrimp docks. Not everyone here has one, though. Or else, because the night is so hot, some have chosen to sleep on the ground outside. Each of these fallen bodies is bordered by an assortment of suitcases, shopping bags, wire-wheeled carts. A few of the men are still up, sitting by a small charcoal fire with a piece of screen laid across it. Some small fish are popping and splattering on the screen. The men are passing around a bottle. They're all smoking. It looks like a smoking contest. As Mrs. Crooks gets out of the car, one of them shouts over to her, "Hey, Iris, how's about a little nookie?"

Another pantomimes beating off.

"Real gents, every one of them," Mrs. Crooks says to Lacy, then reaches in across the front seat and shakes her hand. "It's been a pleasure."

Lacy watches her go to a box a ways off. She has to get down on all fours to get through the cut-out doorway. Once inside, she pokes her head out and waves goodbye.

Lacy gets as far as the street and then pulls over and presses her forehead to the top of the steering wheel. She stays like this for a while, punching the radio pushbuttons on the dash of the ancient Camaro as if trying to dial someplace that has no number. Then she heads home to talk to Franco. He'll be asleep, she knows; the Stations always knock him out. He wakes up fast and alert, though. And listens.

When she's finished, she says, "So...?"

"I'll ride back with you," he says.

When they get to the shrimp docks, Lacy leaves the engine running so Franco can listen to the radio while he waits. She gets out and goes over to the box, and then hesitates a moment over correct form. Knocking on cardboard seems a ludicrous application of politesse, like English castaways wearing their bowlers and vested suits on a desert island.

She pokes her head in. Mrs. Crooks is propped on a laundry bag, reading by the light of a candle a copy of *People* with

Hugh Grant on the cover. She doesn't seem particularly surprised to see Lacy.

"I'd like to get a subscription," she says, "but they won't deliver out here. They don't consider this an address."

"Why don't you come back with me for the night?" Lacy says. "I've got a spare room."

Mrs. Crooks mulls this over, then nods.

"It's been a while since I've been a houseguest. I'll just get a few things together." Actually, everything is ready to go. She hands three shopping bags out to Lacy, grabs the laundry sack and an old belted suitcase herself, and the box is empty except for the old piece of pago pago that covers the ground. On her way out, she licks two fingers and snuffs the candle.

She hesitates a moment when she sees Franco in the back seat. Lacy motions her on.

"My brother, Francis," she says, hoping he'll just act normal in this little introductory moment.

Instead he puts the fingers of his right hand limply in the air and gives Mrs. Crooks his blessing.

"Thank you most kind," she says, swinging her bags into the back seat next to him, then climbing in the front next to Lacy, adds, "Your brother's got a little priesty number going, I see." When Lacy starts up the car and gets rolling, Mrs. Crooks leans over and puts her cheek down on the door frame, closing her eyes and pressing her face into the wind, like a happy spaniel.

Around noon Lacy wakes up, alone and glued to herself in a sweat on Franco's couch. *Lawrence of Arabia* has rewound and spit itself out of the VCR. She pads into his kitchen, takes a cup from the Mr. Coffee, which has been on awhile and has reduced the coffee to thirty-weight sludge. After taking a sip, she beats on her chest with her free fist.

"Ooogah," she says, doing a gorilla impersonation to no audience. She goes upstairs to her part of the house and pushes open the bathroom door, forgetting she has company. Mrs. Crooks is occupying the tub. She nearly fills it with how much of her there is. Lacy notices a serpent tattooed around her left breast. It's an elaborate picture, freighted with symbol. The snake is clenching a rose in its jaws, has dice shaking from its tail. There's more detail, but Lacy doesn't want to gawk.

"Don't be a stranger," Mrs. Crooks hails her in. Considering how little access she's had to indoor plumbing, she is extremely fastidious. Every morning that she has been here, she's taken a Jean Harlowy bath and has about run through what bubbling salts and scented oils Lacy has around.

"How did you clean up when you were..." Lacy tries for tactful phrasing, "...in transit?"

"It's harder up north. Missions'll sometimes give you a dunk, but there's usually delicing down the line. Down here, it's easier—what with Nature's Bath, if you get my drift." She gestures vaguely off in an Atlantic direction. "Of course, with the ocean, it's always a bit of a trade-off—dirt for salt and sand. Not like a tub." She pats the porcelain side.

"Do you have any relatives? Anyone you want to let know you're here?" Lacy says. She tries to make these questions sound like an offer of help. But, of course, they come out of a vision she has of a large car pulling up between the lemon trees that border the driveway. Some variant of "family" emerging. A worried daughter. A Mr. Crooks, perhaps. Someone who folds Mrs. Crooks into their arms, then into the back seat and then off the horizon of Lacy's responsibility.

Unhappily, these questions do not elicit the desired response. At first, they merely tangle Mrs. Crooks up in thought or memory, then finally launch her into a sad, looping saga.

"I've got a sister somewhere, but I can't find her anymore. She travels with circuses. In Mexico mostly. She has an act as The Headless Woman. It's all a fake," she assures Lacy, then sighs and pushes herself up and out of the tub, pulling the stopper out with a deft toe maneuver. Lacy hands her a towel, then flips down the toilet seat and sits. "I've got a daughter that's a lemon," Mrs. Crooks goes on. "She's been saying yes to drugs. Worse, she's attracted to the lowest sort."

"Oh, I know what you mean," Lacy says, about to strike a chord of response with reference to friends dating guys who can't commit.

Mrs. Crooks nips this in the bud, holding up a hand to show that Lacy does not know what she means.

"Once, before he croaked, she told me she was thinking of writing to Richard Speck in prison. She'd seen his picture in the paper, thought he was kind of cute."

This stops Lacy in her tracks, and she sits silently while Mrs. Crooks reaches for the talc and shakes a storm of it over herself. Lacy is seized with coughing and covers her head with the damp towel in self defense. Mrs. Crooks lifts it and peeks inside.

"Sorry," she says, then lights a cigarette and sets it in the groove on an old plastic ashtray she has put on the sink. She goes on. "I had a little house. It wasn't much to begin with, and then they moved the tanning factory in down the street, and so I hardly got two nickels for it, but I gave them both to Darlene. So's she could start in a rehab program and then get some computer schooling. Mothers want to believe, I guess. Of course, she took it and bought junk. This fella she's with now's a stone junkie. Tried to stab me one time over a toaster oven." She turns to Lacy, naked and serious, hands on cellulite hips. "Never play bingo with junkies."

Lacy nods as if making a mental note of this, then asks, "Where'd you go when your house was gone?"

"Well, I was working then, as a domestic. For a very gracious lady. I lived in, until she died. Then I couldn't find another job. For golden agers, the career options trim way down. I went to unemployment, and they found me something, but it was two hours each way. I couldn't keep it up. I was living with a friend then in her apartment. What a place. The landlords wanted us all out so they could rehab and raise the rents. So they ran wild dogs through the halls at night. You looked forward to your nightmares for a little relief. I wound up in public housing, which was really an old hotel. If I told you about that place, you wouldn't believe me. My days was all lines and sitting in colored plastic chairs waiting for forms or checks or stamps or cheese. The papers are full of stories about how the housing and welfare system is a big flop, but I think it's really quite a success— if you understand that the main point of it is humiliation."

She looks at Lacy until she is sure she comprehends. "So anyway, I booked. Took to the open road. Never looked back."

Lacy watches as Mrs. Crooks pulls her stretch pants off the towel bar where they're puckered next to Dr. Munoz's examination jacket. She tries to remember how much she has in her checking account. Not enough. Of course, there is always the Visa company, with whom she has an ever-deepening relationship.

"I was thinking maybe you could use a few new things," she says, trying not to sound like a samaritan. "I could pop." For replacements, Lacy is thinking of cotton sundresses at the Lovely Lady Frock Shop, but Mrs. Crooks is firm about going to Jog Togs out at the Key Lime Mall, where she picks out a running suit, two tank tops, a T-shirt that says BODY IN PROGRESS, and a large, baloony pair of shorts.

"I favor the leisure look," she tells Lacy.

On their way back through the shopping center, Lacy figures she might as well press for a haircut. She doesn't expect to have much success. She assumes anyone with hair three feet long has a vested interest in long hair, but apparently this is not the case. They go to a walk-in cutting place with a ten-dollar special. Mrs. Crooks asks for "something Annie Lennox." The result is a crewcut style that makes her look a little like a rabbit. She's surprisingly good-natured about it.

She looks almost regular now. Franco oohs and aahs when they get back. Lacy can tell he thinks they're performing a missionary function, retrieving a lost soul, but she worries they're just charging Mrs. Crooks a ticket price into civilization.

Harry Windsor is in Lacy's studio, looking at the paintings in the "Modern Myths" series, which is now finished. Lacy doesn't want to jinx anything with her presence and so is sitting in the kitchen, having a glass of wine to slap down a few neurons. She wonders if Harry will think she's an alcoholic for drinking at three in the afternoon, then remembers that he used to have espresso and two lines of coke for breakfast in the days before he tested HIV-positive and his T-cells started dropping like flies. Now he leads the life of a monk in a religion of self-care.

When he comes back into the kitchen, it's as though someone opened the door of granny's oven. It's his aftershave, which has a nutmeg cast to it. It's the only sharpness about him. Otherwise, he's eerily smooth. His hair is fine and light, thinned to chick fluff on top, cut elsewhere in tiny overlaps, like the feathers of an adult bird. His shave is always close; his face appears poreless. His eyes are pale blue, the lashes blond. Everything about him is rounded—chipmunk cheeks, sloping shoulders, high convex belly. His voice is foggy. Lacy finds him erotic in an outerspacey way.

"Well, you've got your show," he says to her now, as though tossing her a beach ball of happiness. She catches it with a wide smile, closes her eyes, and throws her head back. She thinks, *It's the very first moments of any happiness that are the best.* Before the caring sets in—whether the success will bring money, if the passion will last, if it will be sunny when the plane lands in Paris. In this case, what will set in is the understanding that she's not succeeding on terms that mean much to her. Still, she supposes it's better than failing on terms that don't mean much to her.

She has gone back to working on her riskier, probably totally unmarketable work, stuff that has no ironic aspects. All these paintings—there are five so far in various stages—are abstract in technique and concern women in stances of power. These are not paintings young, double-income couples would want hanging over their sofas. She wonders what Harry would say if she showed them to him. She imagines he's adept at making artists feel their work isn't good enough when it's really that it's not commercial enough. Then again, these paintings might not only be uncommercial but also bad. She doesn't have her usual points of reference to fall back on. At any rate, she's not ready to show them to anyone just yet. After these few years of easy if puny success, she's terrified of failure, also in a less investigated way, terrified of genuine success. And so for now, she's content with small safe success and afternoon kitchen celebrations. She tells Harry,

"I've got a bottle of Pouilly Fumé in the fridge."

"None for me," he says, holding up a warding-off hand. "Do you have any spring water?"

"If you consider the kitchen tap a spring of sorts."

"Thanks, anyway," he says, then looks around. "Is Franco home?" Harry is intrigued by Franco's reclusiveness. Franco is intrigued by Harry's smooth manner. They sniff at each other like dogs from different blocks. Franco thinks Harry's a CIA operative. It could be that Harry is attracted to Franco, although this probably wouldn't be reciprocated. Franco—in the abstract at least—seems to be interested only in women. His religion sanctions sexual freedom, but his personal priesthood demands celibacy. Lacy suspects he falls short of the mark, though. Sometimes he stays out overnight. When he comes back, he performs mortifications of the flesh. Sometimes—usually when Lacy has company—he thuds his way up the wooden back stairs, on his knees. This takes him nearly forever. Other times he takes walks with pebbles in his shoes. This confines him to small, tentative steps, like those of a recent stroke victim. There are also odd diets and fasts. Once she noticed that his sheets were sprinkled with sand.

He never says what sins these atonements address. The few times Lacy tried to pry, she was made to feel like an annoying jack-in-the-box and was gently pushed back in, the lid tapped shut over her head. She guesses he's trying to get something right and having a rough go of it. She wishes he'd bring some of this stuff to her because although she can see that there might be a certain internal neatness to confessing to himself, then turning around and granting himself forgiveness and absolution, she worries that this will ultimately spin him into some profound isolation of the soul.

"He's golfing," she says to Harry. It's a lie. Franco is upstairs, but she knows he won't want to be disturbed. He's in the middle of a translation job. Assembly instruction for do-it-yourself Japanese stereo components. He knows nothing about stereos but still gets quite a bit of work from this outfit. What they like is that he can translate so it sounds like someone Japanese wrote the instructions. This and a customer relations phone number in Osaka gives customers an edge of hopelessness about calling with problems that come up.

She opens the wine for herself, pours a glass, and takes it and Harry out onto the glider on the patio.

"Is this the beginning of my meteoric rise, do you think?" she says.

"Could be. On the other hand, the show could be a flop and you could wind up a laughingstock around town. Or you could get famous with these paintings and never be able to do anything as popular for the rest of your life. You could spend the next fifty years as a has-been, like Justine Carrelli."

"Who's she?"

"*American Bandstand.* Danced with Bob Clayton. Seventeen was her big year."

"That's a good boy. Bring me down a little," Lacy says.

"Nah. Stay up there. This is one of the good parts."

When he's gone, Lacy brings the wine, her glass and an extra into the spare room, where Mrs. Crooks is taking her afternoon nap. She has been here for a couple of weeks now. She shows no signs of leaving, but then she shows no signs of staying either. Every morning, she takes her suitcase and goes out. Early in the afternoon she returns for her nap. If she goes out again at night, she packs up again. She never leaves anything behind except for a note, which she props on the dresser. It reads, "Thanks for the Southern hospitality." When she gets back, she takes the note off the dresser and puts it away. It is by now getting limp and smudged and curled at the corners. As charades go, it's quite an effective one. Lacy has not yet been able to think of a way to ask someone to leave who is always already leaving.

The blinds are shut when Lacy goes into the room. The old air conditioner stuck in the window is wheezing wetly. Mrs. Crooks accompanies it with arythmic sleep noises. She snores and sputters like some vaguely malfunctioning small appliance—a nacho cheese melter, an automatic pancake flipper. Something Marc Morgan might have marketed.

She's sleeping on top of the spread in one of her tank tops and shorts, which reveal vein-webbed thighs. She lies spread-eagle across the bed. Knowing that waking her is only slightly less arduous than raising the dead, Lacy takes a direct tack, pressing the cold bottle against Mrs. Crooks's bare arm. Her body remains still, but her eyes pop open.

"Have some wine with me," Lacy says, rinsing the glasses out in the adjoining bathroom. "I'm going to be rich and famous."

Mrs. Crooks nods as though she understands, even though she doesn't. This is a good thing about her. She sits up while Lacy pours. She reaches into her carryall on the floor next to the bed and pulls out a sample pack of cigarettes. She has a seemingly endless supply in different brands. Lacy can't remember ever seeing her with a regular-size pack.

She takes the glass from Lacy and swallows the wine with a wince.

"Sour," she says.

"It's not pineapple," Lacy says, referring to the wine Mrs. Crooks buys for herself and keeps in the refrigerator. The bottle comes wound in plastic netting and has a toy parrot tied to the neck.

Mrs. Crooks abandons the glass on the nightstand.

"How famous?" she says.

"Not very."

"My husband was a painter."

"Mr. Crooks?"

"No. Another one. I forget his name. He painted houses."

"How could you forget the name of someone you were married to?"

"Well, I'm using the term loosely," Mrs. Crooks says. "Anyway, the fumes got him in the end. Painters. They all go off their heads sooner or later. It might already be too late for you. You might already have the start of a big cancer growing in there." She bugs out her eyes while poking an index finger illustratively at the side of her head.

Lacy wishes Mrs. Crooks was turning out to be a little more charming.

Helen and Marc are in Miami for the day, connecting to a seven port-o'-call cruise of the Caribbean. Cruises are a way for Helen to travel. She had a stroke a couple of years ago, and it left her right leg a little gimpy, so stalking around Egyptian pyramids or across the Himalayas are no longer options.

Lacy and Franco drive up to meet them for lunch. Their cruise doesn't leave until seven at night. The restaurant is called—about twenty years too late—Bobby McGee's. It's Marc's choice; a business buddy recommended it. It's one of those places where the water comes in mason jars and the salt is on the table in its tubular blue carton and the pepper comes in its big, square, red-and-white can—straight from the grocery store. The attitude of the place seems to be young and hip, but most of the customers are older, retired types. The few young people who are there are so aggressively youthful—roughhousing at the bar, rumpling each others' hair across the tables—that Lacy suspects they've been brought in by the management as atmosphere enhancement. Like those fat trout they stock tourist ponds with.

Helen and Marc are already there. They're always early. Lacy can't remember ever beating them anywhere. They never look like they've been waiting, though. They always have an air about them that someone's delayed arrival has only given them a wonderful, unexpected little bonus of time with each other.

Marc is standing up, pressing his napkin to his thigh, motioning them over with his free hand. As usual, he has gotten a great table—a big booth in the back. Although over these twenty years he has stepped pretty gracefully up in class, slid pretty neatly into the image of business personage— reversing to dark suits with light shirts, exchanging Italian slippers for English brogues, letting the blond in his hair replace itself with gray—there are still a few vestigial tics from his sharp-guy days. He still carries too much cash, and in a roll rather than a wallet, still snaps off twenties, creasing them between the fingers of headwaiters and hostesses. Laying down a little carpet of goodwill, heightening everyone's assurance of a seamlessly good time.

"You guys look great," Lacy says, and means it. She sees they're both a little heavier, but it sits well on them. Marc is in real estate now; making money in large, quiet exchanges. They drive a soft-riding, boatlike Mercedes, listen to light classical music on a stereo with state-of-the-art noise reduction. They have an uncomplicated social life composed of old, old friends and duplicate bridge. This cruise is a bridge cruise. Marc, along with a lot of the others, will probably not make it off the ship to see any of the ports o' call. He's close to being a Life Master, needs only a few red points, which this floating game will be large enough to provide.

Before Lacy and Franco can sit down, there's a round of hugging made awkward by Franco's physical shyness, by the booth, and by Helen's not being able to get up easily. The four of them look like a social traffic accident. When they're all finally seated, Helen heaves her bosom in a sigh (Lacy notices that what she used to think of as Helen's huge breasts have resolved themselves into a monolithic bosom), and says, "Well."

Tossing the ball into everyone else's court. She punctuates with what used to be her great smile—full of expectancy of delightful occurances. Since the stroke, though, a few tiny muscles around the right side of her mouth no longer do their part, which gives the smile an odd deadness, a quality somewhere between falsity and emotion withheld. Lacy isn't used to this yet, always gets caught short by this expression, then adjusts to it, compensates in her mind for the smile she knows Helen is trying to make.

"You kids want something to drink?" Marc says, raising his hand, bringing the waiter immediately with a fast, nearly inaudible finger snap. Lacy asks for a white wine, Franco for a red.

"Some shampoo," Lacy says, pulling a gift for Helen from her shoulder bag. "From the aloe factory. For your cruise." It's a little gift pack, green plastic netting holding small bottles of shampoo, conditioner, lotion.

"Oh, how nice," Helen says. Lacy can't tell if she means it, or if she only uses beauty products from some obscure European spa and will give this package to the chambermaid as soon as she unpacks on board the ship. Even when Helen is flat out lying, there's no way to tell. A lifetime immersed in the polite codes of the North Shore has enabled her to eradicate even the faintest ring of insincerity from her tone.

"Here." Franco has a card for Helen. This is a surprise to Lacy, who holds her breath while Helen slides a half-inch peach-painted pinkie nail under the flap and opens it.

"Oh, sweetie. A spiritual bouquet. Just like the old days." She shows it to Marc. "A hundred Our Fathers, Hail Marys and Glory Bes—all for my intention."

"Said and done," Franco says. "Transferred to your account, as it were." He gestures in a vaguely upward direction. Lacy closes her eyes. Marc, though, chuckles as if Franco is being a witty guy.

They want to know how Lacy and Franco are doing. In great part, this is a code for money—that is, do Lacy and Franco need any? But the price of them knowing the truth would be their worry, which neither Lacy nor Franco want. And so they fluff themselves up. They tell about Lacy's show, of course. They say Franco has a big translation job.

"Oriental manuscripts," he says seriously. Marc and Helen listen, and relax into all this PR, nodding and smiling. Lacy wonders if they're really buying it or whether the four of them are just all working under the tacit assumption that what's told will be accepted as truth and will therefore be of equal operative value. The way people trust their dollars without rushing down to Fort Knox to see if they are really backed with silver or anything. As long as nothing looks too peculiar, it's easier for everyone to leave the harder questions unasked. (Before they leave today, Marc will slip Lacy and Franco a check that pushes precisely against the upper limit of what could be considered "gift," just shy of what would have to be acknowledged as "helping out.")

It's a nice lunch. The food is good, despite an overclever menu. Lacy has the Surf & Surf, which is two pieces of fish, yellowtail and red snapper. It comes with small clumps of carefully cut and arranged vegetables and fills her with resolve to begin fixing real meals with components, and balance between food groups.

"We have a little announcement," Helen says, patting Marc's hand, bridelike. But they're way too old for that announcement. Lacy can't think of an announcement age has not placed them beyond.

"We're moving," Helen says. "Into the city. We've sold the house and bought a loft."

Lacy is stunned. She can't imagine Helen detached from the suburbs, from her Cape Cod house with its Early American kitchen and French provincial furniture.

"What about your garden?" she says. She can hear she's kind of whimpering.

"Oh, sweetie, I'm just so tired of keeping everything up. After so many years, the whole place has become a stone around my neck."

"Where is this loft?" Lacy says. She can hear that she sounds like the father of the teenage girl asking the date, "Just where is this party?"

"It's called Printer's Row. It's near the Loop. It's a very hep area."

"Hip," Marc says.

"Yes," Helen says, then to Lacy, "I guess we just want to kick up our heels a little."

At first, this strikes Lacy as an odd choice of image for someone who uses a cane. Then on second thought, it seems not odd at all.

"We'd like to plug into the city a little more," Marc adds.

Lacy hates herself for feeling churlish. She just assumed Helen and Marc would always stay put, souvenirs of her past, gathering dust on a sunny window sill. Not off kicking up their heels, plugging into things. Still, here they are, announcing a high-energy future, and Lacy can't stop being stupidly standoffish and petulant. It's Franco who gives her a way off her high horse.

"Hey," he says. "I mean, it's just so cool of you." He smiles radiantly, like a rheostat getting brighter. Lacy sees him making a circle of his thumb and middle finger as he pulls his hand away from his wine glass, a sign that his fingers have touched the Eucharist. He must have consecrated a piece of the stale French bread from the stupid tin breadbox in the middle of the table. She reaches over and grabs the hand with her own in a gesture she hopes will pass for joining in his well-wishing. Actually, she's forestalling him from giving Marc and Helen his blessing, which won't be necessary in the middle of Bobby McGee's.

"We've been going through things," Helen says, leaning over to pull something out of the enormous leather bag she has next to her on the floor. "You know. Getting a fresh start. We can't do that if we're dragging everything we own right along with us. I've cleaned out both your rooms. I saved whatever looked like you might kill me if I got rid of it. Next time you come up, you can have a look. I found this on the shelves in the library." She pulls from the tote an old photo album, fat with past. She puts it on the table. For a moment, it sits there exerting more presence than anything or anyone in the restaurant. It's as though it's ticking. Finally, Franco takes it and opens it on the table in front of him. Instantly, he's too fascinated, looks at each photo for way too long, and then finally gets stopped dead by one of the whole family at the old Casa Marina beach.

Everyone's in their bathing suits except Tom Blackwood, who's wearing a seersucker suit. There's an old Buick at the edge of the frame, pulled right up onto the sand. Lacy and Franco are little and their parents are astonishingly, wonderfully young. Their expressions are filled with being young and with the times surrounding their youth. Their faces are free of even the most passing thought that anything bad could possibly happen to them.

No one can say anything while Franco stares at this picture, and the moment becomes excruciatingly long. Lacy reaches over and closes the cover softly.

"How nice of you to bring these, Aunt Helen. We'll have to look at them when we have more time."

At seven, Lacy and Franco—having helped Helen and Marc up with their luggage, exclaimed over the luxuriousness of their stateroom—now stand on the dock waving enthusiastically at the ship in general, although they're not able to see Helen and Marc in particular. It's hugely lit, a celebration of white and light against the deep-blue dusk. Finally, after much lowing of its horn, much rushing around of guys in very white uniforms undoing huge ropes, the ship slides away from the dock to call on its ports. They watch it get smaller and smaller, waiting for it to disappear. Then they see that it won't—that the ship is way too bright for the night to be able to swallow it up. After a while, Lacy says, "You want to go to the bar?" Although she doesn't give it a name, and although it's been twenty years since they've gone there, Franco understands what she means and nods.

They wind around for half an hour, homing in on the right block. The neighborhood is worse than Lacy remembers. The kosher restaurant is gone. Where it used to be, now there's a store selling portable stereos so large it would take a small family to carry one, TVs with pictures so bad it looks like the sitcom they're all playing is being acted out underwater.

But the bar is still there. Their parents' favorite. They'd bring Lacy and Franco along with them, on the way to the kosher restaurant, sit them in a back booth with a deck of cards, and go back up to the bar to sit and josh with the bartender and watch the cartoons—enlarged panels on a reel-to-reel strip that crawled behind the bartender's back. Naughty cartoons. An anachronism in the nineties, but amazingly, they are still here. Lacy thinks they may be the same cartoons. The hairdos on the busty mermaids being chased by shipwrecked sailors are French twists and pageboys, the secretaries taking dictation on their bosses' laps have lips that are lusciously red, pursed. Franco used to cover his eyes, even in the back booth, and then confess to having come here, just to be on the safe side. Now, though, he watches the cartoons pass. The album sits unopened on the bar between them

Lacy orders a couple of drafts. The bartender at first seems to be the same guy their parents used to kid around with, but then Lacy realizes this is impossible, he's not much older than she is. It's just the past replacing itself, which it does in Miami in a particularly depressing way. Whenever she wanders a little ways off Collins Avenue, onto backstreets of unrenovated hotels, Lacy remembers the old people who used to sit on the painted metal chairs in front of these. They've all died off by now. When she passed by these in the old days, in the back seat of her parents' car, the old people who sit there now were busily rushing through the middle of their lives

"They're so dumb," Franco says, referring to the cartoons.

"Of course. What else could they be?"

"I don't know. Back then, I was too scared to look, I guess. I thought the whole place was a near occasion of sin. It's kind of pathetic—having wasted all that anguish on something so innocuous. Why didn't you tell me they were just dumb?"

"I probably wasn't sophisticated enough at thirteen to know. I mean, I was just a small person drinking a kiddie cocktail."

"Why are we here?" he says.

"I don't know. I wanted to talk to you about them, but I'm not sure what it is I need to say."

"That picture was a jolt," he says. "I had them all redesigned. Enhanced. Colorized. In my imagination, they were older. Older and glitzier. Movie stars. Do you remember how they used to tell us we were a drag, no fun at all?"

"Yeah, we were sober, that was our problem. It's so hard to find kids who are real party animals." Lacy doesn't see them as stars at all. Or younger. They've aged in her mind. They're not at all like Helen and Marc, though. They're a little too loud. Her father wears pants with ducks on them, and his blazer; her mother has lipstick on her teeth. They both still smoke and have wheezy laughs, like Mrs. Crooks. They're Republicans; they're against too much environmental protection down here, and they still call blacks "coloreds," like they don't know better. She imagines having dinner with them at Antonia's, sitting through the whole meal hoping nobody she knows will come in.

Franco takes a sip of his beer, which leaves a foam mustache. He's hearing her out, but she's not sure he agrees with her.

"There's more," she says and looks up to see a naughty nurse pass by on the cartoon strip—you can tell she's a nurse by her cap, which is all she's wearing—in a hospital bed next to a guy whose arms and legs are suspended in casts. Lacy doesn't read the caption. "What does it say about me—about us—that they were so second-rate, so insubstantial? I mean, it's like being a radio and knowing you come from that shop next door. I worry that sooner or later I'm going to run up against my own second-ratedness. I'll walk away from someone who's drowning. I'll become astoundingly famous for painting sad-eyed clowns on black velvet."

"They weren't second-rate," Franco says. "They weren't anything, except drunks. There really wasn't anything else about them in the end. And now they just sit there behind us, filling in all the dead space. They're the brick wall at our backs."

The night of the opening of her show, Lacy is galvanically nervous, a conductor of anxiety. There is always the chance—despite Harry's vote of confidence, despite her pandering to popular tastes—that people won't like these paintings (which would be so much the worse precisely *because* they are so pandering). It seems fate-tempting to just assume they will. And so, in the process of not letting herself get too cocky, she has worked herself up into a genuine state of nerves.

She tries bringing herself down with a childhood trick: imagining the worst. The worst here would be someone spitting on one of the canvases, then saying to her, "I spit on your work." She has never heard of anything like this actually happening in real life. She must have gotten it from a movie. One of those historical dramas about Michelangelo or Goya. It sounds like what the infuriated archbishop said on seeing *The Naked Maja*. The premise of the trick is that imagining the worst will fend it off. Tonight this works; tonight only good things happen.

Jack arrives early, with Mrs. Crooks in tow. Lacy took her shopping earlier in the week to get her an outfit for this. In her size, the possibilities were limited. She chose a stretchy powder-blue knit pants suit with flecks of silver woven through. Lacy talked her into a pair of white sandals over her protests that they made her dogs bark. Mrs. Crooks has had her way in the end. She has left the sandals behind in favor of her tennis shoes with holes cut at the little toes to accommodate her bunions. She is made shy by this setting and wanders off to watch from a corner.

People are arriving in pairs and mixed lots, accompanying their entrances with the thin rushing of silk, the squeak of new soles on old plank floors. They drift in on the aftersmoke of cigarettes crushed on the sidewalk just outside the door.

Some friends, also some strangers come over to pay compliments. After a few, Lacy sees that a lot of these are words that have been rehearsed in the minds of their bearers before being spoken. So what? This may not be her best work, but it is hers nonetheless, and she flushes with every piece of approval she gets. She wants more. This is her little night, and now that it's going wonderfully, she wants to suspend its animation, freeze it in Lucite, lock it forever into the present tense.

She feels confident enough now to scan the room. She watches people dragging broccoli florets through the dip on the buffet table, nicking away at a large pad of brie, drinking wine from plastic glasses with screw-on stems. Amid them, she sees Mrs. Crooks looking furtively both ways then slipping a few slices of ham into her carryall, getting the evening onto her terms.

Lacy turns to look at people who in turn are looking at her paintings. Standing in front of the smallest canvas—*Elvis's Shades*—is a woman Lacy doesn't know, has seen around, though. She's someone who could not go unnoticed on an island this small. She has the profile of the hood ornament on a luxury car of the thirties, and a lot of blonde hair in a hurry back off her face. Lacy wonders if she's Swedish. It's that kind of face, that kind of blonde.

She's not part of the usual art crowd. She hasn't dressed for this as if it were a social occasion. She's just in black jeans and a white linen shirt with the sleeves rolled up unevenly. She doesn't seem to be with anyone or concerned with being seen by anyone. She's not holding a glass of wine. She appears to simply be engaged by the painting. Lacy simultaneously loses a little respect for her, and has an impulse to unbutton the white shirt. She's brought back by the light pressure of hands on her shoulders from behind, and turns. It's Franco in white tie.

"Oh, my," she says, truly surprised.

"I want them to think someone has flown in from Biarritz for this."

"They'll just know you're my brother, but thanks, anyway. It's still terrific."

"Who is she?" Franco doesn't miss much.

"Don't know. Maybe I'll get up my nerve and go find out."

Harry comes and leads Franco away to meet a Japanese woman, who supposedly speaks little English. Lacy looks for Jack. He seems to be enjoying himself with Margaret Nye, whom he knows from the old days on the art fair circuit. Margaret découpages pictures of grandchildren onto the wooden tops of basket purses bought by grandmothers. Lacy turns back to look at the blonde, who now appears to be transfixed in front of another painting, *Neil Armstrong, Composing Moon Greeting*. She threads through the crowd. When she gets to her, she can't think of anything to say, and so just stands behind her until the woman turns.

"Are you the artist?" she says, not at all Swedishly.

Lacy nods.

"I don't have the vocabulary to talk to you about this," she says, waving a hand to encompass all the paintings. At first, this seems a slightly dismissive gesture, then Lacy sees she's dismissing herself. "It's wonderful, though."

"If you think it's wonderful, I don't care about your vocabulary." They talk for maybe three minutes, during which time

Lacy manages to go from dead-idle to fifth-gear. As soon as she realizes this, she's awash in embarrassment. The woman is looking at her with plain amusement.

"I have to go," Lacy says, waving a hand vaguely toward responsibility. "Have to." She's half hoping the woman will put a delaying palm on her forearm, say something arresting. But, of course, she only nods and lets Lacy walk off.

"So who was the androgynous blonde?" Jack asks her the next day.

"Shane somebody," Lacy says, as though she doesn't remember a last name, which is Naughton and is written, along with a phone number, on the inside of a matchbook in the pocket of the jacket hanging on the back of the chair across the room. "She tends bar at Louche. She wants to know more about art. Art. We're supposed to get together for lunch. You know. We won't."

A surprising card arrives in the mail. On the front is a photo of a wall lined with pay phones. On the inside is written, *You could call.* —*Shane*

This makes Lacy feel both exhilarated and as though she wants to sit under the kitchen table and hide for a few days. She lets the card go unanswered. Also the message on the phone tape a few days later—*"Or on the other hand, I could call you."*

She rewinds and shuts off the machine. She goes back to the kitchen, passes the spare room and looks in. Mrs. Crooks is sitting in the canvas butterfly chair reading *People* and soaking her feet in a plastic pail of something purple and murky. This is a preface to paring her bunions. Her treatments, like her ailments, are both disgusting and dated, malaises people don't have anymore. Or if they do, they call them by modern names and have them scanned with rays, excised with lasers, rather than self-diagnosing and attempting to cure them at home with salves and poultices and plasters.

Mrs. Crooks has no truck with doctors, but does a lively commerce with druggists. And even from them she doesn't buy anything mainstream like Contac or One-a-Day. Her products are back-of-the-store, top-shelf items untouched by modern marketing. Jars of drawing salve, bottles of Rudolf's Pine Tonic, boxes of Fleebert's Manila Power, pills good for two or three seemingly unrelated ailments like backache, pin-worms, and weak nails. When the complaint is more general and vague, she goes to someone who does not operate out of a drugstore. From this freelancer, she buys live leeches. Lacy has already decided to go to the movies on leech night.

She looks up, motions Lacy into the room, over to the bed. "Take a load off."

"What's new?" Lacy says, nodding toward the magazine.

"Roseanne is happy at last. With this latest guy. This time it's for keeps."

"I can't read that stuff. Their persistence of belief gets me down," says Lacy, who is restless and cynical lately. Even the most insipid love songs on the radio—even those sung by Whitney Houston—make her hit the station buttons to get away from all the reflection and rumination they start up.

"I think it's kind of inspirational," Mrs. Crooks says. "How people can get decked so many times and still bounce back. Like Eddie Fisher. I thought he was down for the count romance-wise, but then I read he finally found true love."

"Oh, God. Eddie Fisher. Hasn't he been at it too long? What's it now—thirty or forty years? Debbie. Liz. Connie. Who knows who after that? Just imagine all those flowers and long-distance calls. And then the boredom, the escape. The courts and the settlements. Then getting it together for another round. Oh, boy. There must've come a time when he wished he had it all on tape so he could just run the loop for the next one."

"You got logus of the bogus or something?" Mrs. Crooks says. She pulls a foot—white and puffy from the soak, miss-ing only the identifying tag around the big toe—up onto her lap. She opens her pocket knife. Lacy gets up to leave.

"You need something to pick you up," Mrs. Crooks says. "Soon as I'm done here, why don't we go over to the Crab Cottage? Tonight's all-you-can-eat shrimp. I'll treat. I worked the Casa last night and some soused broady left me a twenty."

Lacy hates the Crab Cottage, but she doesn't want to insult Mrs. Crooks. Coming from her, the invitation is a huge overture.

Once there, Mrs. Crooks eats three plates of shrimp to Lacy's one, then orders a fourth, which she dumps into a plastic bag inside her beach tote. The waitress eyes her with suspicion. Lacy would like to go through life without being tossed out of the Crab Cottage, but there's nothing to be done. All she can do here is Fay Wray a little, sit on the bed in the hotel room, look out the window, and try not to be astonished that King Kong is tearing up Manhattan.

Later that night, after Mrs. Crooks has fallen asleep in front of MTV, Lacy shuts off the set and goes out into the backyard and lies in the cool grass. She thinks about how sometimes the future is fog-bound and you can see only the next few steps. And how other times—like now for instance—it's like an opera and you can see all the scenes and acts through to the dying at the end, and understand all the labyrinthine plot twists even though they're going to be sung and in a foreign language to boot. Still, even surfeited with all this libretto, which ought to keep her safely flat on the overgrown lawn of her backyard, Lacy says, "fuck it" into the night, and gets up damp and grass-stained and goes inside to change and head over to Louche. Just for a drink—although she has never been there, is usually asleep for three hours by this time.

The place is packed with women, the air charged with possibility. Trepidation hits Lacy in the knees, a circuit activated between nerve and cartilage. She stands near the door, back in the crowd, so she won't be found. She wants to watch without being seen. Otherwise, she's working with no net, coming on with all the obliqueness of a two-dollar valentine.

Shane is in high gear—a study in motion efficiency and stream of friendliness. Eventually she looks up from sloshing glasses through the wash sink, looks back down, then back up through the crowd, at Lacy, who collapses into relief, realizing she did want to be found after all. It's not quite the smile she was hoping for, but close. She works her way up to the bar.

Shane waits and asks what Lacy's drinking. Lacy completely misses the question, stands stunned, as though she's been asked to come up with an answer that requires the application of logarithms, or a fluency in Wollof. She's half a beat behind before they've even begun, dancing to her own reggae of romance. Shane likes this.

"My guess," she says, "is that, just in off the street as you are, you're not quite ready for an upside-down margarita."

Lacy face looks puzzled.

"You sit with your back to the bar and lean your head back onto it and open your mouth. I pour in a shot of tequila and a dash of lime juice, then rub salt around your lips."

"Oh, I'm not nearly there."

"Then I'll fix you a chi chi. It's a good drink for the not nearly there." When she brings it back—it's milky and comes in a stemmed glass—she says it's on her.

"I don't get much opportunity to patronize the arts." She looks at Lacy dead-on and says, "Plus I'm surprised to see you."

Lacy, inappropriately, nods. She has a mouthful of chi chi which she's trying to swallow. It seems to be made of evaporated milk, Nutrasweet and Mrs. Crooks' pineapple wine. When she gets it down, she says, "Well, you made the place sound like a lot of fun. I was just on my way back from somewhere. You know."

"I don't think you're making it sound casual enough," Shane says. "You should put in the part about getting a flat tire just down the block and having to come in and use the phone to call for a tow."

"Yeah. Well," she says brilliantly.

"Hey," Shane reaches out and pats her hand. Like an aunt. Like the person in the seat next to someone flying for the first time. "I've got last call now. It gets kind of nuts from here on." She backs off, wiping her hands on a bar rag, then travels down the bar and locks into deep eye contact and seemingly significant dialogue with a woman at the other end.

At home Lacy gets a bottle of cran-something from the refrigerator and goes into the studio to stretch out on the yellow sofa and feel miserable. When she wakes up, she's not sure how long she's been asleep, or why she's so suddenly awake, but she thinks there was a noise. She holds still and listens. It's there. Creak-squeak, creak-squeak it goes. Out on the small patio just beyond the sliding glass door. Someone's on the glider.

Lacy gets up, deerlike as possible, goes over, parts two slats of blinds with a metallic snap, and looks out.

It's Shane. She's lying the length of the cracked oilcloth cushions, one sandaled foot on the ground, to push herself off. Little pushes. She doesn't seem to be waiting for anything.

Lacy raises the blinds with a slow pull at the cords, then slides open the glass door, which has a plastic frog suctioned to it, to show birds and drunks that it's a door.

"How'd you find me?" Lacy says, panicking a chameleon with the dusty sound of her bare feet on the tiles as she comes out.

"Asked around."

Lacy nods. Shane stands and stretches and comes up so close Lacy can feel breath on her cheek, the rolled-up fabric of sleeve grazing her arm.

"You want to come in?" Lacy feels this is a reasonable offer, given the context, but Shane seems startled at its boldness, or its unseemliness.

"Oh, no. Can't. Got to be somewhere."

Lacy tries, but cannot bend this into good news. Shane is either lying to make a quick getaway, or she's someone who's expected somewhere—probably not the library—at four or five a.m., whatever time it is. Or, worst yet, she's just one of those girls with a restless, pointless energy that sets the planet a fraction of a degree off its axis.

But when she says, "So. You think you could come by tonight? I could fix dinner? You know."

Lacy hears herself say yes, and then closes her eyes for an instant and sees the life of sweet reason disappear in the rearview mirror.

Lacy knows that hearing about Shane Naughton will make Franco nuts, but she's determined to bring up the matter right away. That was her mistake when she was starting up with Jack. She wanted to break Franco in gently and so for the first month or so, told him that Jack was the new termite-control person. This made it only worse in the end. This time she's going to tell him from the start, which is probably now. Besides, she can't not. She desperately needs to say the name to someone. Shane. Shane Naughton. My new friend Shane Naughton.

Also, she needs advice on how to proceed, how to push this off the ledge of something that might happen. She's been reading the letters between Virginia Woolf and Vita Sackville-West for clues, but it's hard to pull much of practical use off a flirtation conducted through freighted telegrams and literary luncheons, passion consummated at a country estate. Franco's a much likelier source for ready-to-use tips, because of his addiction to *Love Connection.*

He's practicing chip shots in the backyard. There's a hole with a flag pin stuck in it at the far end. His "par two minicourse." She drags a lawn chair over to his tee, where he's standing next to a mixing bowl full of battered golf balls. He's wearing yellow plaid pants and a purple polo shirt. He thinks the clothes are one of the best things about golf.

She sits down with her cup of coffee.

"Do you remember the blonde at my opening?" she says.

He keeps his eye on the ball, but says, "I think it would take severe amnesia to forget the blonde at your opening. I think she would be what a person forgot just after he forgot his address, just before he forgot his name."

She waits for him to swing. The shot misses the pin by three or four feet.

"I was doing better before you came out. It's the main thing keeping me from turning pro and getting on the tour—my bad reaction to gallery pressure."

"She's asked me over to her place for dinner tonight."

"A new friend." He's already getting weird. She forges on anyway. She's not going to cave in.

"I think maybe the invitation's for dinner and after-dinner."

He turns and arches an eyebrow, like George Sanders.

"Come on. Help me."

"You've been out to dinner before. You're thirty-seven years old. What can I tell you?"

"But maybe it *is* just dinner. Maybe she's straight. I don't want to make some mistake that turns this into a black-bordered page in my diary."

"Why is it I had the idea *you* were straight?" he says. "Maybe it was all those guys hanging around. Maybe it was just something you said."

"Please."

He leans forward against his golf club and thinks a moment.

"I'll give you a Valium. Pop it just before you go. It'll take you down a couple of notches. To regular. You don't want to show up at the door with hives and swallowing your tongue."

"That was last night. I went over to Louche. She tends bar there. What I had in mind going in was being incredibly cool—sort of like me, only played by Sharon Stone. What I wound up with was autism. I'd like to do a little better tonight."

"It's hard for me to come up with anything directly applicable. On the *Connection,* it's all straight. They never, you might have noticed, have lesbians on the show. I don't think Chuck could handle it. And most of the guys seem to go for women who have that Glenn Close kind of look. Frizzed hair and husky voices. But I don't know if you could really make that work for you. I'd just say, be yourself."

"A Valium and be myself. Great."

"Hey," he says, tapping her foot with the putter. "Seductions are easy. It'd be much harder if you wanted to be popular at parties. Then you'd have to learn to play the piano."

S tanding on the wooden porch of the old two-story conch house on Olivia Street, Lacy is jazzy. She presses the top buzzer, next to the Dymo tape stamped NAUGHTON. The response is fast-thudding footfalls and then Shane in gray sweat shorts and a maroon T-shirt with the sleeves cut off. Lacy is in wrinkled white linen shorts and a navy polo shirt. She changed three times before defaulting into this outfit, which now seems a little too yachty. The bottle of wine she's holding cost five dollars more than she usually pays. All of a sudden she feels queasy with foolishness.

Shane slips a finger through a belt loop and leads her back into a kitchen where there has been a coup. Garlic has taken over. A pan of chicken pieces is under siege in splattering oil. She slides the finger out and uses the hand to lift a corkscrew off a nail in the wall.

"Why don't you open that while I finish putting this together, and then we can sit down and get drunk."

"Then you might forget the chicken," Lacy says.

"Sometimes that happens," Shane says and smiles and pours a can of tomatoes into the pan, making the oil seethe.

Then she adds a can of mushroom soup. The recipe is on the label. She checks it frequently, as if it were the life support monitor for a critical patient. It looks as though this is the third, maybe fourth meal she has cooked in her life.

Lacy looks around the kitchen. On the wall is a blowup of a snapshot. The scene is a birthday party. The birthday girl is an eight- or nine-year-old Shane, surrounded by friends. Girls obedient for the flash, boys edgy in plaid sports jackets and clip-on bow ties—all of them perched forward on chrome-legged, plastic-seated kitchen chairs around a Formica-topped table. They're toasting Shane with raised glasses of milk as a woman in a small-print dress, a pearl choker, and a tight permanent bestows a white-white cake before them. This picture is no less telling for having been hung ironically.

The corkscrew is of no kind Lacy has ever dealt with. She gives up after a while and is about to shrug in defeat, but Shane has already seen the problem.

"I'll get it," she says, and when she has, she pulls two water tumblers off a bracket shelf of raw wood. "Well, you look terrific."

"I worked at it a little," Lacy says.

"I deliberately didn't. I guess it comes down to the same thing."

They eat at the kitchen table off plates of different patterns, with silver liberated from someplace called Ellington's. It's engraved on the handles. In addition to the chicken, Shane has put out little Waldorf salads topped with maraschino cherries. Lacy thinks how you hardly see maraschino cherries anymore. A garnish of the past. Maybe working in a bar, Shane thinks of them as a respectable member of the fruit group. There are also rolls. Lacy can't taste any of this. She's way too far outside herself—observing from an eerie distance—and at the same time way too deep inside the experience to have any normal, regular sensation of the meal. Shane seems much calmer.

"I love this part," she says, but doesn't elaborate. She gives a little background. She's been down here four months. Before that she was living in Boston, taking classes—she doesn't say in what, working in a boutique. "The Blarney Stone. They sell only Irish stuff. Oily sweaters and plaid blankets. You know." She tells Lacy that she writes poetry. She gets up and goes into the living room and brings back a construction-paper covered, stapled-together pamphletlike affair titled "Invisible Footprints." Lacy thumbs through. She knows hardly anything about poetry, but can tell this is really awful. Shane seems to be moved by summer storms, walks in the woods, holding hands with someone while watching the sun come up, and simultaneous orgasms. The poems read a lot like personals ads done up by an eccentric typesetter.

"They're so touching," Lacy says, who really is touched that Shane would make herself so vulnerable by showing the poems, particularly since they are so terrible. Then, putting the chapbook down and patting it gently, Lacy takes the first subject jump she can find. "They make Boston sound so romantic. Why'd you leave?"

"I don't know. Stuff up there started to seem like it was going to count on my permanent record. I needed to get someplace where I could just be temporary for a while."

"A lot of people come here thinking that," Lacy says. "And then one day they look up and notice they've been temporary here for ten years."

Shane nods a little too long, assimilating the heaviness of this remark. Lacy gets embarrassed for her.

"Do you have any coffee?" she says.

"Or I could bring out another bottle of wine," Shane says. "Not as good as yours, but bigger. Or we could roll a joint."

"Yes," Lacy says.

"The correct answer."

The living room is small and lit up with a spectacular dying sun flooding red through the jalousie windows at the front.

There's no furniture per se. Futons are folded against two walls, meeting at a corner. Scattered around on them are pillows of different sizes sewn into pastel cotton sacks. Like a practice space for tumbling clowns. As they set themselves adrift in here, Lacy decides she likes this notion of decor. At the same time, she suspects that, had she found the arrangement in the apartment of someone she liked less, she'd probably think it precious.

They lie side-by-side. They're lightly looped by now.

"I love it down here," Shane says. "I've been meeting so many interesting people." Lacy knows she doesn't mean "people." When you work all night in a women's bar and spend your days tanning at the Coral Reef, the only people you meet are dykes.

"And now I've met you," Shane says.

"Another interesting person."

"You bet," Shane says, sounding like a mouseketeer. "When I wrote about you in my journal, I put red highlighter over your name."

Lacy would kill to see this journal. As she's trying to imagine it, relaxing into the out-of-real-time quality of this conversation, Shane, in a panther move, flips over onto the palms of her hands and balls of her feet and begins doing slow pushups over Lacy, stopping just above her on the downstroke, not quite touching. And she does this without smiling, without blowing off the gesture even the slightest bit. She looks straight at Lacy. But Lacy can't meet her earnestness nor her eye, and turns her head.

"Hey," Shane says, making her turn back and look up into dead earnestness. "I guess what I'm saying is do you want me to make this easy? I can do that."

Lacy nods and Shane lets herself down the rest of the way. She's slow, deliberate, sure, locomotive. Lacy lies across the tracks.

A couple of light-years later, Shane looks at her in the flat white moonlight overlaid with wavy blue from neon outside the window somewhere, and says, "What're you thinking?"

"I was thinking that you're the most wonderful person in the world, but some of that, I realize, is probably the moment. By tomorrow I'll probably have come down to thinking you're just the most wonderful person on the island. What're you thinking?"

"That first night. At the gallery. I was turned on the minute I saw you."

"Yes?"

"Oh, yeah. Famous artist and all, everyone kind of hovering around you. It was hot."

Lacy doesn't know which is worse—that Shane is attracted to something as shabby as celebrity or that she thinks Lacy is one. There's a fast little trapdoory sensation underneath her heart as it occurs to her that, for all the big emotion she's going through tonight, this is probably third-rate romance. She remembers the Sunday morning one of the girls in the Providence boarding house came back and told the rest of them how romantic it was that they put a little coffee machine on the bathroom wall at the Atlasta Motel on the highway out toward Boston, and did they think true love was possible with someone if you weren't sure whether his last name was Schuster or Schuler?

O n her way in, Lacy stops off to see Franco. It's nearly eleven in the morning, and he will have missed her by now.

He's bent over his writing table, like a watchmaker. Writing is close work for him. His script is small and neat. He fills page after nearly marginless page through long silent weeks of many drafts. When he has a verse in final form, he transfers it in a thunderous bout of typing on an aged electric so large and noisy it seems that it must be performing two simultaneous functions. As though it must be a typewriter/punch press. A typewriter/pinsetter.

What he's working on is a rock opera on the transubstantiation. He has been working on it for more than ten years now. He hopes it will illuminate for the world, the mysterious changing of bread and wine into the body and blood of Christ. He feels terribly pressured about finishing. It has to be performed by the Stones, and if they break up before he's done, he says he'll just have to scrap it.

He looks up. At first she can tell he's not seeing her. Then he reenters her dimension. She sits on the bench in front of his electronic keyboard, unwraps a hot dog she picked up at Aunt Lolly's, holds it out to him.

"No thanks," he says. "Boy you look awful. Like one of those women who move to Rome after their third divorce so they can just sit in cafés and hold still and not have to make any more big mistakes for a while."

"I just got up too soon."

"Ah, I forgot," he says, although they both know this is unlikely. "Well? Did she seduce you? Did you seduce her?"

"I think it was too close to call."

He doesn't say anything but gives himself away with a bit of blinking and a hard swallow. He's fighting back tears. Lacy hates herself for upsetting him, especially when it would be so easy not to. She could just tuck this thing with Shane—if it even is a thing—into some corner. That's what she's done before, with Jack and the few others before him. She made sure that Franco wasn't disrupted by any of them, made sure he always had the upper hand. She tried not to bring them around much. She'd go out, stay out even, but when she came back, she'd trash them a little, smile at Franco's withering criticisms. She doesn't want to do that this time, though, and so is having to watch the panic surface. He's afraid she'll abandon him, run off and leave him out of coffee filters, on his own to deal with the Hinckley & Schmitt man who scares him, alone to make his own phone calls and appointments, which take him hours to work up to.

She wishes she could tell him this won't happen, that she'll never leave—but she can't. The fact is that she'll always stay because he can't be left on his own. If this knowledge were moved from tacitly understood to spoken, it would—she's sure—slam an impossible, insupportable weight on her side of the delicate, complicated equation they've worked out between them. They'd never recover from it.

And because they can't directly assuage his fears of her abandonment, they can only directly confront the possibility that someone else will be the villain, will lure her away. And so this morning, Shane will have to be made into the villain, then whittled down to size. After walking in determined not to do this, Lacy collapses in on her good intentions. She simply can't stand up to the tyranny of Franco's panic, and so offers, "She's a poet."

"Don't tell me," he says, happy, grateful. "It's Yeatsian."

"It might be the worst in the world. At least of poems printed on pages. I mean, not counting poems cross-stitched on kitchen samplers."

"How can you be interested in her then?"

"I just like her. She's nice. She likes me."

"Everyone who knows you likes you," he says, but he's only playing now. He's calm again.

"She said she'd call," Lacy can say now, now that everything's safe. "Do you think that means she really will?"

"Oh, sweetheart, I don't know."

"You mean she won't?"

"I mean you can't know. You don't have enough information. Only bill collectors are sure to call. It would have helped if you could have borrowed a large amount of money from her last night."

"Do you think her saying she'll call means I shouldn't?"

Franco goes back to his lyrics.

Shane walks around Lacy's studio like a Presbyterian tourist from Missouri going through the cathedral at Chartres: quiet, awkward, humble in her ignorance. It's the first time Lacy has seen her since the night they spent together. That was a week ago. During these seven days, Lacy has called her a minimum of four times a day, never getting an answer. Then, yesterday Shane called, wanting to come by and see how Lacy works.

"It's terrific," she says about the studio.

Lacy leads her back into the living part, explaining as she goes about knocking out the walls. "I left the bedrooms. I didn't think I'd want to sleep in a giant dark space. This is Mrs. Crooks's room here."

The door is open. Inside Mrs. Crooks is panting away on a stationary bike Lacy brought in from the garage for her. She stops while Lacy introduces Shane. Then, by way of acknowledgment, she snorts. Or something like snorts. It's a sound she makes that's something like clearing a nasal passage, but which she apparently thinks also qualifies as conversational. Her noises are many, worst when she's cleaning the house, something she's started doing to help out, "on a consultant, as-needed basis." When she wet-mops the floors or scrubs the tub, her face breaks out in pinpoint red dots, her forehead bursts out in sweat, and small groans start emanating from someplace deeper than her throat. At first this was disconcerting to Lacy, but Mrs. Crooks reassured her.

"I like to let it all hang out," was what she said.

Now she smiles suspiciously as Shane says, "Pleased to meet you," moving deeper yet into her Missouri Presbyterian mode.

"My room," Lacy says when they've moved on.

"It's so white," Shane says.

Lacy moves out of the room to continue the tour, but Shane pulls her back in, into some kissing. Lacy is more rattled by this sudden intimacy than she was by the chatty distance that preceded it. What happened the other night was so pulled out of context. Now, here in the dead center of her context, kissing carries weight.

Shane mistakes the source of the nervousness.

"Is that your mother in there?" She nods toward the whir of the stationary bike.

"Oh, no," Lacy says. "Mrs. Crooks is just staying with me for a while." She leaves it at that. Mrs. Crooks's presence is difficult enough for Lacy to explain to herself, much less to someone as new as Shane.

"Then we don't have to worry about parental disapproval," Shane says, winding a foot around behind Lacy, tapping the bedroom door shut. At the same time, she's unbuttoning Lacy's shirt and then unzipping her jeans, giving them a starter tug down her hips.

"Get them off," she says.

Later in the kitchen, when Lacy has poured glasses of iced tea with fat lime wedges in them and shaken some Lorna Doones from their package onto a plate between her and

Shane on the table, Franco comes down in a cassock and shower sandals. Lacy makes introductions.

"I just wondered if you got me some more Mr. Bubble. I'm out, remember?"

"I forgot. You can use my Vitabath for now."

He nods. She and Shane watch in silence as he disappears through the doorway, shower sandals thwapping, reappears with the plastic bottle of Vitabath, points at it as though he's in a commercial, then thwaps down the back stairs.

"Your brother," Shane says, not unreasonably. "Is he a priest?"

"Sort of," Lacy says, hoping this will do.

"Maybe you'll want to talk to me about your life sometime," Shane says. She is not being sarcastic.

"Of course."

"It's just that my own family is so boring. Just above plant life. My parents run this little insurance agency. They go on vacations in this giant rec vee. Inside, it's just like their house, only smaller. It's not roughing it or anything. Everything in the kitchen has a quilted cozy over it—the toaster, the blender, the juicer. What I mean is that I'm not just being idly curious. It's just that everything about you seems so much more interesting than anything about me."

"Oh, you're pretty interesting," Lacy says.

"I'm kind of a type. You just haven't been around much."

Mrs. Crooks snags Lacy in the hallway outside the john while Shane is still sitting in the kitchen.

"Watch out," she whispers loudly. "That one's a lezzy. I can spot them a mile away. From my little times in the slammer."

Lacy can't think of anything to say to this.

"She's not putting the muscle on you, is she? For ciggies?"

"I don't smoke," Lacy says.

Mrs. Crooks nods distractedly, already a worry or two down the line.

"Right. Well, just keep a sharp eye out."

Franco waits until late that night.

They're watching a video he picked up. Vanna White showing her celebrity hair and make-up and fashion tips.

"Most important, though," Vanna is saying, "just be yourself."

"See," Franco says.

Lacy nods. She's stretched out on the floor in front of the set, now closing her eyes, giving over to sexual drift.

"She dresses like a weirdo," Franco says from up on the sofa where he's sitting cross-legged, peeling a mango onto a paper plate on his lap. Lacy opens her eyes and peers at the screen, confused.

"Vanna White?"

"Your girlfriend," Franco says.

Lacy turns over and glares up at him.

"That's right. You come into my kitchen looking like a papal nuncio in a steambath and you're telling me she dresses weird. You can really afford to set yourself up as an arbiter of style."

"I know that a T-shirt and a vest is not a style. It's Ed Norton."

She reaches up and yanks his big toe.

"Hey. I thought you were working on jealousy. On your imperfection list."

"It was just so *thick* up there. In the kitchen."

"We were having *cookies,* for Christ's sake," she says, then realizes she was swearing. "Sorry."

He nods. The phone starts to ring upstairs in her place. She leaps off the bed and makes a faster run for it than is really decent.

It's Shane, calling from the bar.

"I don't want to be here," she says and laughs.

"I'll come by and fetch you when you get off," Lacy says.

"You'll still be up at two-thirty?"

"Probably not."

"What're you going to do? Set an alarm?"
"Something."
"Oh, baby."

It seems Jack's mother is finally near the end. To look at her, it's hard to believe she's still alive, that she still has enough steam to open her lids in the morning. She has lost most of her healthy weight. Her skin is thin and shiny; it looks like a light loose nylon carryall for her bones.

She's in the hospital now. Lacy went yesterday with Jack. At first, walking into the room, Lacy couldn't find her amid all the machines she's connected to. It's clear she's never coming off these machines. Maybe if she were a hardy young dockworker who'd gotten in a scrape with a loading crane. But she's a seventy-eight-year-old woman, and the machines in this room are locks through which she's being lowered into deeper waters.

Later she and Jack go for a swim off the seawall behind his house.

"Swimming these waters in the summer is kind of like meditation," she says. "The water's so close to your own body temperature, it's like slipping into another layer of yourself."

He gets out a couple of rafts and pumps them up, and they float side by side as the sun slides down toward the horizon.

The mosquitoes start to come up, but he seems not to notice. Lacy doesn't mention them, doesn't let go of his big hand holding hers. She's trying to do a decent job of being around. She's been here for two days. She'll drive back home later tonight. She wants to get to Louche by closing and drop a big net over Shane. She doesn't tell Jack this, of course. She has only mentioned Shane to him as someone with whom she has been having lunch, although so far they have had no lunches together.

   She's not particularly trying to lie. The truth just seems like way too much information at the moment.

"What are you thinking?" she says later when he's standing next to the wall phone in his kitchen. He has just finished talking with his mother's doctor—blood pressure numbers, medication adjustments, the small talk of ineffectuality. Nothing that will matter is left to be done.

"I'm thinking," he says, coming over, sitting down across the table from her, "why can't she get a break? She's said all right to dying. She's being a sport. So why can't she get a last week or so of fun? Nothing wild; I'm not thinking of a rush off to the Taj Mahal. Nothing that would violate parole. Just a little reprieve. She could do some of the things she used to enjoy. Work on her lime trees. Sit by the seawall in her old chair."

They go out on the back porch, which is a new, decklike replacement for the sagging old verandah. The raw wood hasn't been painted yet and smells sweet against the salt mist. He hasn't been interested in sleeping with Lacy. It's as though he's hooked up to his mother, like one of the machines. They sit in the light from the sunset, which is simultaneously red and cool, and look out over the gulf. Lacy looks up, projects herself into the near future. She already misses him.

The morning after Lacy comes back down from Sugar-loaf, Shane calls. She wants to cheer Lacy up. Lacy has to take a whole day off. They'll play tourist.

They go to the beach, rent a raft, and buy Italian ices from a wagon. They stay long enough to play all of Lacy's Bob Seger tapes on her boom box.

"Bob Seger might be the voice of rock and roll," Shane says.

"My brother would disagree. He'd say Dee Dee Sharp was probably the voice of rock and roll. The harbinger."

"Tell me about the guy up on Sugarloaf," Shane says.

"Jack."

"Yeah. Make me jealous."

"Well, I've known him for a couple of years. The romance never really took off at the beginning, and so we've just sort of kept running along the ground. What can I say? He's a nice guy." She starts to say he's a terrible painter, but holds back. She doesn't want to betray him to Shane. She's already betraying Shane to keep Franco happy. She'd like to not become a completely terrible person, like Dorian Gray, her portrait rotting in the closet.

"If his mother weren't dying, would you have told him about me?"

Lacy nods, but Shane is on her stomach, her face pushed into the elbow crook of her arm.

"Are you nodding yes?" she says in a muffled voice.

"Yes."

"What about your brother? Have you told him?"

"Sort of. Why?"

Shane lifts her head and slides on her sunglasses to really look at Lacy.

"Because if you're telling the people in your life, it's a good sign for me."

Lacy's heart pumps with hope.

They walk back down Duval, crinkly with sand and salt. They run into Heather and Claudia, and stop on the sidewalk to make a jumble of introductions, a little flurry of small talk. Lacy hasn't told Heather about Shane yet and can see her surprise. The conversation seems particularly effervescent, as though Shane is a fountain in the gardens behind the Villa D'Este in the hills above Rome and Lacy is able to show her off to Heather in this perfect late afternoon light that slants to her best advantage, revealing her rainbow complexities. At least this is how Lacy sees the exchange. She realizes it might be a little less heady for everyone else.

She and Shane continue down Duval. They buy each other red T-shirts that have HEARTTHROB stenciled on them, slashily written inside an off-center heart. The saleswoman who wraps them up has long nails polished purple. She looks through her long, mascaraed lashes at them, as if this foolishness is a shirking of the serious business of husband-hunting.

At Shane's, they shower.

"Come on," Lacy says, getting Shane out. "You'll drown if you try that in here."

The apartment is thick with the accumulated heat of the day. As Lacy lies naked on the cool terrazzo floor in the living room, Shane brings in iced sun tea. They drink a lot now from a single glass, share sandwiches by alternating bites. At the ice cream place the other night, Lacy let Shane feed her rocky road by small spoonfuls. She would retch if she saw two other people doing this.

It seems that all her time lately is taken up with making love with Shane or thinking about it or traveling in a punchy haze of having made love through all the hours she should have been getting sleep. Everything between them now is either sex or sexual surround. Her skin and lips feel tender and puffy, her mouth dry, her eyes heavy-lidded. All this must show, she knows. She feels disengaged from the larger world; coming into it, she is surprised to find things still rolling along as usual. Coming out of Shane's venetian-blinded bedroom into rude daylight, she marvels that other people are going about buying ironing-board covers and car insurance and onions. Keeping dentist appointments. Eating francheezies in snack shops.

Even her work is suffused with Shane. No longer working on anything remotely salable, she is absorbed in private, personal canvases whose subjects have softened. Her powerful women now float in sunlit pools gone white like beds, and in beds at dusk, gone blue like pools. She is not at all sure whether this is the bravest art she's ever made, or complete trash—sex-by-number painting.

Working on one of the first mornings after one of the first nights with Shane, she gets stopped by a flash of recognition. In an instant, the whole of the summer with Pam Fields comes tumbling down on her. She has not felt like this in twenty years. It's exhilarating, releasing only for a second. Then merely terrifying.

One night Lacy dreams she is swimming in a pond behind an old deserted mansion. The lip of the pond is velveted with thick moss, the water still and bronze in the sunlight. Tom

Blackwood is sitting next to the pond in an overstuffed chair. He is about the age he was when he died, but Lacy is as old as she is now, and so in the dream they are contemporaries.

"I'll watch you dive," he tells her, and then the phone rings even though there is no phone in the dream. Lacy has trouble surfacing; half-awake, she reaches across the bed, picks up the receiver. It's Heather. She's calling from an outdoor pay phone. Lacy can hear the applause of waves in the background.

"Where are you?" Lacy says, looking at the clock on the floor next to her bed. It's nearly four.

"The beach. Can you meet me?"

"Where?"

"You know the pavilion—where the old guys play chess?"

Lacy takes her bike over. Even riding fast, even wearing just shorts and a camisole, she can't find any coolness. It's August and the nights give little relief. They just feel like black afternoons.

When she gets to the beach, she toes off her tennis shoes and walks barefoot out onto the sand, which is taking a pounding from heavy night surf. Heather is waiting, smoking, sitting up on a railing in a T-shirt and rolled-up pajama bottoms.

"You okay?" Lacy says.

"Oh, yeah. Just burning off a few vapors."

"Claudia," Lacy says.

"She wants to stay with me, but not sleep with me anymore. She says she's become interested in the possibilities of focusing energy through celibacy. She says she's been reading up on this, but I haven't seen any books. I think it's just a smokescreen. I think she's grown tired of me."

"I don't think it's that," says Lacy, who thinks it's probably that.

"You don't have to say anything. I just needed to not be with her, and not be alone for a while. Tell me about Shane Naughton."

"It's so surprising," Lacy says.

Heather rolls her eyes.

"I'm such an easy read?"

"You've just had a look to you for a while. Like Deborah Kerr in that old movie where she's a missionary nun. You looked like she did at night, hearing those jungle drums."

Lacy sticks out her tongue.

"Hey. Let me just be happy you're finally coming over. You must feel at least a little terrific yourself—relieved and ecstatic and all that."

"Not exactly. I'm kind of ecstatic and at the same time feel like I'm going to throw up. I feel like I'm walking around with all my clothes off. Everyone can see everything about me. Especially she can see everything about me." Lacy stops and then starts again. "There was someone else. A million years ago. She dropped me, from a great height. I never wanted to feel that bad again. I've worked at it. Now I've given over all that lovely control. Now I'm hostage to the Fates again."

"It doesn't have to be this harrowing," Heather says. "If you find someone goodhearted and steady on her feet."

"Oh, no. You don't like her," Lacy guesses.

"She's terrific to look at."

"There's a fatal flaw. You know something about her that I don't."

"Just her bad reputation. She's a heavy-hitter. If you were asking my advice, I'd advise against this. Nothing against vulnerability, but you've got to pick your spots."

Lacy nods.

Heather nods.

"My, but I'm being sensible and tiresome." She walks over and puts an arm around Lacy's shoulders and pulls her cigarettes from the waistband of her pajamas and lights one up, then puts it between Lacy's lips and holds it for her to take a drag. As though Lacy's a dying infantryman in a World War II movie.

Lacy stands at the kitchen counter slicing an avocado. She's fixing supper. She's trying to get the household on a healthier tack, fresh foods instead of frozen or carry-out.

Mrs. Crooks is even worse in this department than Lacy and Franco. Left to her own devices, she'll eat just Fritos and Little Debbie snack cakes. She's suspicious of this new plan.

"What is it you're fixing exactly?" she says. She's sitting at the old bleached wood table. Her legs are stretched onto another chair, one arm flung over the back of the one she's sitting on. With the finger of her free hand, she's pressing down on the holes of the salt shaker, picking up loose grains and then licking them off the finger. And then repeating the process.

"A salad," Lacy tells her. "There's not enough going for you in corn chips. You need other stuff. Fruits. Protein. Vegetables."

"Corn's a vegetable," Mrs. Crooks says. She's pretty punky for an old person.

"Corn's a yellow vegetable," Lacy says as if talking to a second-grader. "You need green and red ones too."

"And beige foods, I need those. Pecan Sandies and biscuits with gravy."

"I'll crumble some roquefort on this salad," Lacy says. "Cheese has a lot of protein."

"Is roquefort like blue cheese?"

"You don't like blue cheese?"

"I like Velveeta."

"I don't think Velveeta's really a cheese. It's not in the refrigerated department in the store. It's just on the shelf. It's a not uncheeselike food product, or something like that."

"My diet's not my problem. I eat plenty. Look at this belly." She rolls her paunch from side to side with both hands. "My problem is I'm not getting enough sleep."

"You're upset about something?" Lacy says.

"It's all the noise," she says, and Lacy begins to see where this conversation is heading. She tries to stop it with the force of her silence, indicating that this particular subject is not open to discussion.

"Like animals," Mrs. Crooks says. "And that gloomy music." She's referring to the records of Gregorian chant Franco plays with the volume on nine, all night any night Shane stays over.

"You'll have to talk to Franco about the music. As for the animals, what can I say? I suppose everyone sounds a little animally in bed."

"Women shouldn't be enjoying themselves in bed with each other."

"Well, I suppose some of them don't."

Lacy is just punking out now, which she knows is stupid. But then, any response to this is stupid. She shouldn't have allowed herself to be drawn in. Now Mrs. Crooks is on a roll.

"You think you can give me a bath and a salad and you've saved me. But I've got standards. In the streets I might see a lot, but I can always walk away from it. Here I'm trapped night after night next to all this deviance." She has begun to cry. Lacy discounts this; Mrs. Crooks's emotions are always close to the surface. She cries or laughs the way other people sigh or yawn.

"You're not stuck here any more than you were on the street," Lacy fixes her with a hard stare. "You can book any time."

"Maybe I will," Mrs. Crooks says.

Lacy sets the salad on the table.

"Here. Eat this. I took the cheese off yours."

She is determined not to let this conversation get to her, but she already knows she'll ask Shane if they can spend more nights over at her place. When she does, though, that night, Shane shakes her head.

"We stay here, and keep on doing what we do, everything. We just don't make a sound."

"I can't not make a sound."

"Sure you can. Get into the music," Shane peels off her tank top and nods downward, toward the heavy chords of the Agnus Dei filtering up through the floorboards. "Pretend we're nuns, doing it in the convent."

There are roses on Shane's kitchen table, cut way down so they can be stuffed into a large coffee mug. Lacy stares at them too long. Shane, at the refrigerator, shrugs.

"Occupational hazard. You're friendly. It's mostly just pushing for tips. Sometimes people misunderstand."

"She brought them to the bar?"

"She was waiting outside at closing." By not saying anything more, Shane says just what Lacy does not want to hear.

Lacy watches her pull an old piece of cheese—it looks like rubber joke cheese—from the refrigerator, and a bottle of ginger ale. She gets some crackers down from a cabinet. The silence is holding too long. She drops the crackers on the table, comes over, and puts her arms around Lacy, linking the fingers of both hands at the small of Lacy's back.

"I'm not trying to make you jealous."

"I know," Lacy says. "That's what makes it so gruesome."

Shane refuses to linger on unpleasant subjects, changes this one by pressing an open mouth against Lacy's neck, and moving her hands up inside the front of Lacy's T-shirt, tracing circles on nipples with fingers wet from the soda bottle.

"Oh," Lacy says, breath and fight taken away at the same time.

Shane's looks throw her off. She hates how much they shape and color her feelings. They make her give Shane the benefit of way too many doubts, inform all other interest in her with a slightly lurid subtext. They make her fear her own values are meretricious. She asks herself: if Shane weighed two hundred and fifty pounds and had pockmarks, would she find it kind of cute that she starts phone calls by punching "Heard It Through the Grapevine" on the Touch-Tone buttons?

There's a trash fantasy fulfilled in loving someone who looks like a movie star. But onscreen beauty is distilled in myth, the process kept out of the frame. With Shane, Lacy gets the panoramic shoulders but also sees the bench press in the bedroom, the rack of running shoes in the closet. She gets all that blonde, but also a view of Shane's bathroom—a tabernacle of aloe and jojoba. It undercuts the beauty a little, Shane's awareness and concern. A better person would be more dismissive, she thinks.

Shane has no interest in dismissal, though. She flaunts her narcissismn, riding in on her looks as if they're a huge, sweating horse. Sometimes this taints Lacy's appreciation, makes her fear she's becoming a conspirator in an essentially shabby concern. Other times, though, Shane's voluptuous self-love is persuasive. Admiration seems to fall short, genuflection seems more appropriate.

Shane is not her given name. It's a revision of Sharlene, who was prosaic and expendable and now exists only in the land of driver's licenses. Shane inhabits a world of women whose names either are, or sound, made-up. Anathea. Laurent. Mari. Through stories Shane tells her, Lacy is discovering a whole subculture that spends its time tinkering with persona, perfecting attitude, and conducting superficial but extremely complicated relationships in great part through late-night phone calls. These stories are interesting.

114

The stories Shane tells on herself, though, are chilling. Something icy slides through Lacy when she hears them, like when she first heard campfire ghoul stories like "The Hookman," or "Johnnie—where's my *liver*?!" A lot of the really chilling ones aren't even stories, just dropped remarks. Dropped, as in anvil.

"I've learned," she tells Lacy, "never to use first names in bed."

And:

"I knew Aurore had to leave me to grow. In the end, I had to buy her a suitcase."

The theme has variations. The suitcase for Aurore appears in another story as the necessary change in phone number following Jasmine. Always implicit in these sagas is that this is different. In the (shrinking) rational part of her mind, Lacy thinks that's probably not true. She suspects they were all different while they were going on, only became the same when they were over. She worries she'll wind up in a similar anecdote told to a future lover. Worse, that she'll deserve to be in the anecdote, that this will turn her into someone who will eventually need to be outfitted with luggage or restrained with the help of AT&T.

Shane is draped and layered, shirted and socked in her past with these others who came before. Whenever Lacy compliments her on something she's wearing, it's attributable to a former lover. The way other women say they got it at Sak's or Lord & Taylor, Shane says, "Lenore gave it to me." Or "It's Tara's."

This firms up Lacy's resolve to never give her anything to wear. When it's all over, she doesn't want to be the blue crewneck. And then she gets tripped up when Shane turns around and gives her a silk shirt she can't afford at all. And this happens in the afternoon of a day that started with Lacy waking, sure Shane was going to leave her.

And so when the inevitable happens, it still takes Lacy by complete surprise.

Shane is unavailable. She doesn't call. When Lacy tries, there's no answer, or she's just on her way out and will call as soon as she's back, then doesn't. Once, another woman answers and says Shane is in the shower. The next time Lacy calls—after taking two days to persuade herself that the woman was a visiting cousin—Shane picks up against some background hilarity, belaboring the obvious by telling Lacy that she has company, whom she doesn't identify any further.

Finally, Lacy can't paint. A first.

It's a little past one in the afternoon. The day is cloudless and high-winded. Shane is probably tanning over at the Coral Reef with her crowd—bartenders and waitresses who work through the nights, sleep through the mornings, and lie out together through the better afternoons gossiping and riffing, making up their names, flirting in baseball caps and bikini bottoms.

Most of them are on a circuit. They come down to Key West in the fall, go up to Provincetown in the spring. In the high seasons, they make a thousand or two a week and spend it as fast. It's a high and temporary life. None of them expects to live it for very long. Some of them have plans—computer careers, girlfriends with whom they're going to buy farms in Wisconsin. But for the moment it's all on hold for a liquid life that requires only good looks, an even tan and lots of attitude. Lacy doesn't have enough attitude to play well with them. She always slips too far over some unseen line. Expressing interest too ardently, appreciation too visibly. And then sunglasses are slipped on, cigarettes lit, bodies turned to tan the other side.

She gets on her bike and heads over to the Coral Reef. On the way she tortures herself with visions of what she'll find. Shane spreading Bain de Soliel on someone's shoulders. Sharing a joint under the pier, passing the smoke from mouth to mouth.

She locks up the bike by the far end of the pool and walks slowly down the path alongside the elevated deck. And Shane is there. She's alone. She looks to be asleep on her stomach. Lacy stands looking at her, reeling. In an instant, she realizes that jealousy doesn't need to be fueled by competition. She can stand here and be made insane just by witnessing Shane's ability to lie on a white chaise over blue water, clean winds whipping the corners of her towel against her legs, sleeping peacefully in the sun, breathing evenly, unstricken by pains in the chest. Even though she has not spoken to Lacy in three weeks.

The next time Lacy sees her, a few days later, it's at a show of Heather's sculptures at a place on Simonton, in what was first a church, then a Buddhist temple, then a day-care center, now a gallery. Lacy has brought Jack to celebrate his mother's remission. Two days ago, she sat up in bed and asked for a tuna melt. The doctors are certain this good spell is temporary, but it still seems like an unscheduled holiday.

The show is of Heather's new project. She has gone beyond chairs, beyond mud. The new pieces form a complete living room. All cut from stone. The furniture. The lamps. The rug. The magazines scattered on the hassock of the easy chair. The living room occupies the center of the terrazzo floor. It's drenched in amber spotlighting within the surrounding darkness. The viewer is held estranged, as if locked out in the backyard at night, peering into the warm interior, which laughs back in cynical coziness, uninhabitable.

Jack is resistant. Lacy picks this up from his silence and his stance.

"Heather has put in a lot of work here," she says.

"It takes a lot of work to fart the 'Star Spangled Banner,'" he says. It's only more pleasant when they agree on art. It's never important.

Lacy thinks this stuff is great. She goes over and tries to tell this to Heather, who is too excited to hear it. She stands before Lacy and nods and works Lacy's hand between her own damp ones, but her eyes are glassy, surfeited. Lacy will call tomorrow and repeat her compliments when she's come down enough to hear them.

Harry Windsor comes up behind Lacy.

"I've been trying to get in touch with you," she turns and tells him. She has decided to ask him to look at the new paintings. She's sure he won't want them for his own gallery, but he's well-connected in New York and, if he thinks they're good, may be able to help her out.

"Yeah, well..." he says, "I was tied up all day." He pushes a starched white cuff up a little to reveal a rope burn, and nods toward an extremely bland looking guy in a suit. *"Rough-Trade Tax Accountants,"* he says. Harry likes to capsule review his life in porno titles. She is a little surprised to find out he is still frisking around in the sexual arena. She wants to ask if he's practicing safe rough-trade sex but can't think of a way to work this into a conversation in such a public setting, surrounded by so many people they know, so many hunks of brie and plastic glasses of box wine. She makes a mental note to talk with him later.

And then these concerns evaporate as Shane appears on the scene, accompanied by someone Lacy doesn't know. With one white flash and soft click of her shutter, Lacy records this woman: presses her fingers to the ink pad, then to the file sheet. Puts her under arrest.

She's young, all leg. Stalks rather than walks. Fashionably rumpled in electric-blue fatigue pants and flak vest, she stands close to Shane, moving around slightly, burning off loose ions. She looks as though she's dancing to music so faint that no one else can hear it. She brushes the back of Shane's hand with the back of her own. A gesture no one sees. Lacy sees.

The girl is a lioness on a leash, too full of raw energy to be constrained by this polite society, now looking around, wondering how to get back to the veldt. Lacy supposes there's not much chance of her being desultory in bed.

Jack is unaware of any subtext. This is his first night out in several weeks, and he's ebullient just to be standing here with a drink in his hand and the company of three women who are neither related to him nor dying.

Now the girlfriend has turned to talk to someone else, giving Lacy the chance to ask Shane.

"A new friend?"

Shane shrugs. Her eyes are pure Freon.

"She's the new afternoon bartender. New girl in town. I've just been showing her around." She's clearly bored with having to go through the formalities of lying. Lacy's being tiresome.

Suddenly Lacy knows she's going to be sick. She makes a dash for the john, can find only the men's. She pushes in and throws up in one of the toilets, then sits a while on the old floor made up on tiny tile octagons, pressing her face to the cool marble of the partition wall.

She gets up and splashes her face, then rinses her mouth and rubs at her teeth with a paper towel. They feel like they have nappy fur on them. Then she combs her hair with her hands, trying to fluff herself up from deranged-looking to casually rumpled. While she's doing this, Claudia comes in. She kisses Lacy lightly on the mouth. Her standard greeting. Lacy is never sure whether this is the custom of her country, or carbonation off her casual physicality. "I am hearing you are fallen in love. And seeing your troubles tonight."

Lacy shrugs.

"I know her a little," Claudia says, illustrating with a thumb and little finger held slightly apart. "I am thinking that—for you to love her so—she must have hidden depths. Like a lagoon. No?"

Lacy shakes her head.

"She has no depths. She has only shallows. I have no idea why I love her. I actually sit down sometimes and try to figure it out. But I can't. I am a reasonable person in the middle of a suddenly unreasonable life. I don't sleep. I have diarrhea all the time. I've lost ten pounds. I've spent every moment of the past three weeks in some state of waiting for her to call. I hate myself, and I really hate her."

Claudia smiles.

"So you have joined us mortals. It is good."

"Claudia, how do you say 'fuck you' in Italian?"

"No. I am being serious. We all think this will be, in the end, a growing experience for you."

"You *all*? Jesus. Does everyone know about this?"

Claudia shrugs. "It is a small island."

But Jack lives on another island and misinterprets the problem.

"Maybe I'm vampiring you lately," he says later in bed with Lacy. "I worry that I'm slouching around you too much, wrapping you in my cape, pulling your collar away from your neck with my fingers, pushing my teeth into the softest spot on the curve. I want to suck something from you to make me feel untired. And I realize this is probably not the absolute best basis for a relationship."

Lacy says nothing, and takes the gift of his guilt—space on her side of the bed where she can lie awake while he sleeps. She uses this space as a private screening room where she can run—like an insane editor—again and again, the same clip of Shane releasing the baby dyke from her fatigues. Zippers and smiles.

Two days later—against all the laws of probability—she calls.

"Busy?"

"No," Lacy says, and it's true. She's just been staring at her can of brushes for the past half-hour.

120

"Why don't you meet me at the fishing pier in ten minutes then?"

She's waiting when Lacy gets there. She's standing at the end of the pier, leaning back against the railing. There's a spectacular sea behind her, waves huge and crashy, yet holding their blue—great backup, like the Vandellas.

"I'm sorry," Shane says and slips her arms around Lacy, pulling her in with hands on shoulder blades. "The thing is, it was just going too fast. I needed time to think. Don't be mad. Please. Come on."

They walk back down the pier. Everyone's lucky today. The crossboards are wet with small piles of redfish and sheepshead. A charter has tied up and the mate is cutting tuna—black slicker skin, brilliant red flesh—into steaks.

"I'm not any good at this part," Shane says. "I never get to this part. I rush in and ambush them with roses and Snickers bars and they drop in their tracks. And then I'm embarrassed. For them. For me. And anyway, the point's been made, so it's time to move on. I thought that would happen here."

"But it hasn't?"

"Doesn't seem to have."

"You're scared," Lacy says.

"Oh, yes," Shane says and laughs. "Oh, yes."

Lacy is ecstatic, triumphant. At the same time she knows this moment will have horrible reverb. Shane won't be able to tolerate being this vulnerable for long. Suddenly the uncertainty of the past few weeks doesn't look so bad. As long as she and Shane were pursuer and pursued, they were one step shy of being lover and beloved, two shy of Shane dropping her from that familiar great height. Lacy supposes she should really start now, perfecting a parachute tumble, a fast roll that will let her hit the ground and walk off in reasonably sound shape.

Around three the next afternoon, Lacy comes home. On her way in, she looks up at the sky. Most of the light that's important to her is already gone. Bartenders and painters make badly scheduled bedfellows.

She climbs through the airless stairwell, feeling ghastly, exhausted, auto-piloting on maybe two hours' sleep. It's over a hundred degrees outside. She took a shower less than half an hour ago, but already she feels as though she's been six weeks in some jungle boot camp.

She falls onto the yellow sofa, into her worries. She has almost no money. She has blown off too many days with Shane, worked all of the others on these paintings now propped around the room. They seem quite powerful, but then they arise out of her erotic fantasies, perhaps powerful only to her. She keeps the door to her studio locked now, so no one will see them. At Heather's show, she chickened out of telling Harry about them. If she never shows them, she can always secretly believe she's great. If she lets them be seen, she'll have a lot more hard information on her limits, distant fences she has so far skirted.

"Fuck it," she says, pulling a Coke out of the refrigerator and heading downstairs. It's time for *Love Connection*.

Franco has the blinds shut and his air conditioner humming straight out on high. He looks up when she comes in.

"You'd never make it on as a contestant. Contestants never have hickeys." Then his attention is drawn back to the set. His TV is aged, its picture lurid and flecky so everything looks like it's happening in a vibrant snowstorm.

Chuck Woolery is mediating between a guy and woman coming off a disastrous date. The guy, who has topiary sculpture hair and a confused but earnest look, doesn't see the problem with having shown up an hour and a half late for the date. He was looking for the perfect white rose to go with the black dress the woman told him she would be wearing.

Blown-up larger than life on an elevated video screen, the woman is livid in some backstage holding area. Though she really should only find him hapless, instead she despises him. She's nasal with agitation, vitriolic, probably from encounters with too many previous goofballs. Not realizing how much momentum she's got going, he keeps getting run over by her.

Now she's describing the dinner cruise he took her on—"a barge with gypsies."

"Pirates," he says, as if this will turn her around.

"Good thing they've got this one backstage," Lacy says. "She takes no prisoners, you can tell."

"I think she hates his hair. It didn't look so puffy on his intro tape. What's new with you?" Franco says, casual. She hasn't been home for the past two nights.

"Nothing much."

He keeps looking at the set, and says, "Mrs. Crooks and I went to the dog track last night. We got lucky again."

"That's great. Maybe I'll go over with you next time."

"Get real," he says. He's not talking about her romance, but Lacy saw a three-by-five card of prayer intentions bookmarking his breviary, and so knows he's been praying to Saint

Christopher and Bruce Springsteen, his twin patrons of the traveler, for Shane to move to Arizona.

After the commercial, the contestant is a woman. The guy she picked and went out with is being vicious. Sometimes the *Love Connection* has these days.

"What did you think?" Chuck Woolery asks, "When you first saw Amanda?"

"Well," he says with a smile that's a weapon. "I thought she was a pretty tired twenty-nine."

Chuck turns to the woman, who's sitting solid and unflappable on the banquette beside him. "How do you feel, hearing him say that?"

"I don't have any problem with it," she says, and really looks like she doesn't. A lot of the contestants on this show seem to belong to some sales force of self. They've been on the road ten or fifteen years, showing the same merchandise. A door pushed shut in their face is no longer a big deal.

"She's just my type," Franco says.

Picking women from this show, Franco is fairly consistent in his tastes. The ones who capture his fancy are usually big-boned with hot-roller hairdos, firm beliefs, and no-nonsense attitudes. They appear to be living lives too small to have any room for uncertainty. Often they are nurses, the kind you know refer to their employer as "Doctor," as in "Doctor wants a specimen from you in this cup." Whenever he expresses interest in one of these women, Lacy is always a little surprised. When she tries to imagine Franco going on a date with anyone, she's hurtling into a black hole. She can't really imagine what kind of adult he'd be.

He's getting too thin, his haircut has grown out. Lacy gets swamped with guilt.

"Are you okay?"

"Oh, yeah," he says and smiles. "Everything's going great. I'm nearly done with *Eat My Body.* I've written to the Stones.

124

You know—letting them know. And Mrs. Crooks and I've been winning a bit on the dogs. And He has been making himself a little more accessible. Mysticism is not like other love. It's a by-turns sort of deal—incredibly intense, then terribly lonely. For the moment, though, things are good."

"Let's cop some late rays," Lacy says. "You're getting too white. You're starting to glow in the dark." She's so relieved her absence hasn't been all that important, and now she's ready to pay attention to him. He inspects his arm, nods, and goes to rig up their beastly weather special in the backyard. Side-by-side chaises within spray range of a fanning sprinkler, a pitcher of tea banked in ice inside a styrofoam cooler. He and Lacy sit in old bathing suits and coats of tanning oil, their lips white with zinc oxide. She knows they shouldn't be so phototropic, that they should be heading in an opposite direction of sunscreen creams and wide-brimmed hats. Still, sometimes they just have to tan.

"I dreamt about you last night," he says. "In the dream it's 2010. I've been in a coma for years. You've kept me alive in a machine full of dry ice. Now you've thawed me back to consciousness, and I find out they held the nuclear holocaust while I was out. You take me around to show me. We're in a big city. Everything is leveled. It's all just rubble. But you say you're lucky, you've got a basement apartment. We go there and you put on a record for me. It's not a disc, though. It's liquid neon you pour from a tube onto the turntable. As it goes around making music, it also changes into different shapes. It's playing 'Hotel California.'"

He really does seem happy, if a little weirder than usual. Maybe if she can just orchestrate things a little, maybe if she can bring him out and Shane in, everyone could be happy.

"I think the three of us should get together," she says. "You, me, and Shane. Have tea maybe."

"Can we? Really?" he says, clapping his hands together.

"Come on. It's just a low hurdle."

He thinks for a while, then says, "Well, I could have you down to my place, maybe. Tea and maybe a small Benediction."

Lacy sits up and peers hard at him, then lies back on the chaise and puts her mother's tanning eyecups back on. Franco never has guests. She gets a fast flash of what this small Benediction would be like.

"What a nice idea," she says. "But why don't we just go to the Japanese Garden?"

The Japanese Garden is new and white, an outdoor, gazebo kind of place with purple banners hanging from the trellises. Lacy and Franco get there first. Franco has dressed up in his suit, which is pale-green linen, Armani from a couple of seasons back that he picked up at half price. Under the jacket, he is wearing a black shirt with a Roman collar. Lacy thinks of this as his missionary outfit. He has also washed his hair and combed it straight back. The wet ends curl around the bottom of the jacket collar. Lacy is also wearing green today, inadvertently. A mint T-shirt.

Mrs. Crooks thinks he and Lacy are secret identical twins, that their parents lied to them, but that the truth would come out with really good astrological charting. They don't see any big similarity. They think they look like cousins at most. Cousins with the same basic attitude. They do have the same black hair and gray eyes. And they're both tall and thin, but Franco is scrawny and Lacy's body is a variation on the V shape of muscle and bone all swimmers have. All in all, they think they look extremely different.

"Twins, yes?" the Japanese waitress says to them as she hands them steaming washcloths dangling from a pair of tongs.

Lacy is flushed with expectancy. She thinks the chances of Shane liking Franco are pretty good, if he behaves, which she doesn't suppose he will. The chances of Franco liking Shane are about one in a thousand. Beyond the jealousy factor, Lacy can see that Shane is someone whom, if you weren't in romantic/erotic thrall to her, you could possibly find a little tiresome. So much of her conversation, although charmingly expressed, does center on herself. To truly enjoy her, a person would really have to share this fascination. Which, at the moment, Lacy does. Shane's steady stream of personal lore and facts and preferences (favorite food: spaghetti, favorite color: blue) is a little feast for Lacy. At the same time, she can see that someone else might, twenty minutes in or so, start pounding on the door, screaming to be let out.

Franco nods toward the entrance now. Lacy turns to see Shane coming in looking as though she's right on time, although she has kept them waiting nearly half an hour. She sits down—next to Lacy, across from Franco—and smiles and shrugs and says, "The Mad Hatter, eh? Late for the tea party."

Franco leans back in his chair, then leans forward again. Lacy sees he's prepared a bit of conversation.

"I suppose, being a bartender, you get to be a real student of human nature."

Lacy feels tears starting way at the back of her eyes, behind the retinas. She's stunned by how—even in this tight, stupid little situation she's forced him into—he's really trying nonetheless.

Shane relates an episode that happened at the bar the night before—four friends, very drunk, cutting their thumbs open with a lime knife and declaring themselves Blood Sisters for life. One required a couple of stitches and the others took her over to the hospital, telling Shane and anyone else who wanted to know, that this was precisely the kind of thing Blood Sisters do for each other—take in their wounded.

Mercifully, Franco does not use this as a lead-in to talking about the stigmata, which currently fascinates him. And when the tea arrives, he does not insist on saying a long elaborate grace over it. He stays in reasonably socialized areas—

127

TV shows, rock music. A few times he drifts a little, once into speaking of sainthood as a career goal, another time referring to the sacrament of golf. But Lacy thinks these slide by. The damp spot between her shoulder blades evaporates. She begins to relax. This is, against all odds, going splendidly.

Still, she's really only half surprised when they get home and Franco says, "It's interesting about obsessions. I mean I can see you have breathing difficulties around her, but if you could...well...I don't suppose it's occurred to you that she's someone we'd usually make fun of. Not a lot. I mean she's not hilarious, or completely ridiculous.

As Lacy leaves the room, he's still going.

"...Not like a woman on a house deodorizer ad. More like a girl on a color highlights mousse commercial..."

And she's not really surprised the next day either, in Shane's Jeep, roaring up toward Bahia Honda, when Shane opens the subject of Franco.

"So what's the deal with Dr. Demento?"

L acy goes up to Franco's. He's in his confessional—two old wooden phone booths pushed together, a grille cut between them. As Lacy approaches, he pulls aside the velvet drape and peers out, squinting into the light. He motions her into the penitent's chamber.

She goes in and kneels down. He slides open the door behind the linen-covered grate. He looks ghoulish in the shadows. He's becoming very thin. He swims in his clothes.

"What's up?" she says.

"A couple of things. Something's about to happen, and something has happened. Which one do you want to hear first?"

"What's going to happen?" she says, wary of surprises.

"I know I'm about to get a sign. A response. I can feel it."

Lacy hates this kind of talk. She knows she should be talking with him about his spiritual life, since it really is his life. But she can't. It makes her queasy. Literally. She feels the same way she did in high school. She'd be talking with the nun she had for English, going over a paper and suddenly things would wildly veer off Thornton Wilder and into the reedy marshland of religious talk. Suddenly, Sister Mary Sebastian's part of the conversation would be sprinkled with Christs and Our Saviors and Lacy would begin to itch and feel like the room was shrinking around them, and she had to get out. It's like this talking with Franco, worse even because it's happening in the bright light of now. To Lacy, religion—particularly Catholicism—seems as though it ought to be something color-tinted in a person's past. It doesn't seem to have a place in adulthood, seems almost mutually exclusive with adulthood. That Franco is so given over to it makes Lacy think of him as held back in this anecdotal, sepia-toned place.

And so, "What's the thing that's already happened?" she says, taking a sharp left turn out of troublesome territory.

"Something good about Mrs. Crooks. She wants to tell you herself, though. She has a little celebration planned. She wants us to meet her at the sunset."

"Okay."

He begins to slide the little door shut between them. She thinks he's going to say, "Go in peace."

"Be there or be square," he says. After the door has shut between them, he switches into Latin.

Mrs. Crooks is already on the wide stone steps at Mallory Docks when they get there, sitting amid all the tourists and street performers. She's wearing a new pair of striped bermudas and sunglasses made of little louvers. She pushes them on top of her head when she turns to look up at Lacy and Franco. She has a metal hardware store pail next to her, filled with ice cubes and a huge bottle of Cold Duck. Next to it is a stack of party paper cups. She smiles widely, exposing a two-tooth gap left of center. She nods at Franco.

"You tell her."

"Mrs. Crooks has—through reinvestment and rollover of her winnings at the dog track..."

"Caught a trifecta," she says. "Hit it big."

"How big?" Lacy says, not knowing how far to let her imaginings inflate.

Two hundred dollars is as far as she gets before Mrs. Crooks says, "Thirty-four g's." She licks her thumb tip and does a fast pantomime of riffling through a large wad of bills.

"Thirty-four thousand dollars?!" Lacy says. "You won thirty-four thousand dollars on dogs!"

"Extremely fast dogs," Franco says as Mrs. Crooks pops the Cold Duck cork toward the setting sun.

"It's just so amazing," Lacy rattles on. Even knowing that she's rattling on doesn't stop her. "I've never known anyone who won anything big. It's wonderful. I guess it'll change your life," she says, taking from Mrs. Crooks the paper cup, which is foaming over. "We'll take you straight over to the bank. Help you open an account."

"No, that's okay," Mrs. Crooks says, patting Lacy's hand as though she's said something silly. "I don't like the looks of that bank. It's just a store in a shopping center. I like the old-fashioned kind of bank—big and brickey, with one of those vaults you can see. Besides, there's something wrong about putting dog money in a bank. You have to use your funds in the same spirit you got them."

"Mrs. Crooks would like to use the money to install a pool in the backyard," Franco says.

"The Miami Fountainbleu model," Mrs. Crooks says. "It's a celebrity-type pool. I can show you the brochure. You can get a tile monogram in the bottom, but that's extra. A changing cabana comes with, though. You kids won't have to sit under that woozy sprinkler anymore. We can have splash parties."

There are so many ways they could put the money to more sensible use, but this is not a gesture that would be possible to refuse.

"It'll be the nicest gift anyone has ever given us," Lacy says, and forces herself to kiss Mrs. Crooks just above the sprouting mole on her left cheek.

One morning the next week, Lacy is awakened at seven-thirty by the end of the world, which is being held in her backyard. She pulls on shorts and a T-shirt and goes out on the back steps to see what the apocalypse looks like.

It looks like a steam shovel. A hole is being scooped out of the yard to make way for the Miami Fountainbleu pool. When it's in, she'll be able to do her morning laps right at home. She's been stepping up her workout lately, doing an extra half mile. For these extra laps, she wears a sweatshirt over her suit, and hobbles her kick with foot floats. This has something to do with trying to get inside Franco's mortification, trying to feel what's going on there.

A few days ago, he told her he had begun a meganovena—nine sets of nine days of prayer. Nine to the ninth power. A very powerful prayer in his scheme. The prayer is to Christ crucified, asking for the stigmata, which he's pretty sure he's going to get anyway. The novena's "just frosting."

"He knows I need a sign," he told her. "That I'm operating so much on a set of assumptions that are mostly wild extrap-

132

olations from a single given, and need confirmation. He knows it's the next logical step in our relationship."

"You make it sound romantic."

"Well? If this isn't romance, what is?"

There's been a cool snap this week, signaling the onset of fall. The city pool, with a couple-day lag, has turned cold along with the air. Lacy's swim is more of a hardship. She offers it up, tags onto the mortification laps prayers she hopes will cancel out Franco's meganovena.

She doesn't want him developing mysterious wounds. She doesn't want bleeding to be a part of who he is. She especially doesn't want minicam trucks from Miami TV stations pulling up in front of the house, popping out efficient redheads with hair arranged in serious styles, delivering into their microphones inane summaries that would trivialize him.

She prays that God will instead pay Franco some kind of attention that won't lend itself to being televised.

Shane calls one night around seven. She's starving, has to get something to eat fast, since she starts at Louche at eight. How about a little pizza at the Napoli?

By the time Lacy gets there, they've only half an hour. Half an hour in a brightly lit pizza joint with a thundering jukebox and three college guys at the next table trying to pick them up and Shane half playing them along. Lacy will get little real conversation, maybe a few fast doorway kisses on the way to the bar, all of which will just leave her a roving dog for the rest of the night. Knowing this in advance makes it a low moment. She hates Shane and herself and love, and is glad they don't serve knives with the pizza in this place.

"What're you doing tonight?" Shane says.

"I want to go up and visit Jack. His mother's bad again. He can't leave the house. I play Scrabble with him. I don't know. That doesn't seem enough to do for anyone."

"You ought to cut yourself loose from that deal," Shane says, just before one of the college guys leaps over and tugs his cap onto her head. It's a baseball cap with CRIMSON TIDE on it. They are Alabama boys. Shane flips the cap across the room. "I mean, he's so played out. He's got baggy knees. Where's it ever going to go? You ought to be in something that's got a future."

"Something with you."

Shane laughs. "I'm not even much of a present."

That's it. That's the whole of it. An absolutely plain picture with everything on the surface and in sight. It takes Lacy a week's worth of mental gymnastics to twist it into meaning if she breaks off with Jack, Shane will get serious.

Jack's mother is being buried on Key West. She was a conch, as they say, born on this island. She only moved up to live with Jack a few years before, when she wasn't able to keep up her own place on Margaret Street anymore. The island is an ephemeral place that can't hold its dead any better than its living. The soil here is too sandy, the rains and tides too treacherous to allow actual burial.

Lacy stands with Jack and his family in front of the casket, which will remain aboveground, like all the others in the city cemetery. The dead here are always in evidence, in stone sarcophaguses, or on the shelves of the small mausoleums scattered around the grounds. It's impossible to pass this place coming up Olivia Street—even sailing by on a bike, fresh from the beach—without getting snagged by thoughts of death. And yet Lacy stands in its fat grass today in black sundress, head bowed, eyes cast down, her hair like a mantilla falling around her shoulders, a fraud. She's not thinking about the woman who has just died, nor of death in general, or even of her own mortality. She's running the Shane conversation again and again through her mind, rough-drafting the one she'll have to have with Jack.

She waits until a week or so after the funeral—as if this makes her a decent person. She drives up to Sugarloaf on a Monday morning. He's in his studio, pallette knifing mauve and pink pillows behind the outline of what will eventually be an extremely flattering portrait of the fiftyish wife of the owner of a small chain of trailer parks. In the finished painting, the woman will have much more jaw than she does in real life and will appear to have wisdom far beyond her thirty-five years.

"I think I need to make these cushions a little darker," he tells Lacy. Mrs. Bobbe's dress is a pale pink, and I want a lot of contrast. To feature her tan."

"I can't be your girlfriend anymore," Lacy says, then sees from his expression that this is going to be much worse than she thought. She truly thought this would be an uncomplicated conversation, that if he minded, it would be along the lines of being inconvenienced. Now she wonders how she could have been so thick. And there's no going back on this casual approach, no re-entering the scene wringing a damp handkerchief. By telling him like this, casually, she's made it clear how little value she ascribes to their situation.

"You've met the really terrible someone," he says, although she hasn't mentioned anyone else. She doesn't want to talk about this.

"I know I seem like the kind of person who'll be around when it doesn't work out. But I'm not. I won't."

She tells Shane as soon as she gets back.

"I did it. I broke off with Jack," she says, waking her up, crawling into bed alongside her.

"Oh. I'm sorry to hear that," Shane says sleepily. "I kind of liked him. He has those great eyes that make him look like he's always getting the joke."

Lacy and Shane still sleep together, but less and less often. That is, Shane lets it happen less and less often. Just dropping by is risky. There's a good chance now that someone else will be occupying the guest side of Shane's bed. Lacy doesn't know who the someone else is. The one horrible time she breezed through the unlocked door into this scene, the mystery person tactfully stood behind the partially closed bathroom door. Shane, of course, never referred to the incident afterward.

When Lacy does get to sleep with her, though, she sleeps more soundly than when she's alone, though on a plane nearer consciousness—as though she's in a boat, kept awake by the constant motion, but at the same time lulled with knowing the harbor is a safe one. She wakes at odd hours, passes a light hand over Shane, activating the mechanism that makes her weave her sleeping body against Lacy's, the way a spider curls up when touched with the tip of a pencil. The bed is surface, sides and corners—soft space that circumscribes them in simplicity.

Outside these perimeters, the action between them has become chaotic.

Out of her presence, Lacy suspects Shane gives her very little thought, her version of love based on impulses that visit her randomly, acted on in whatever moment. And that there's no thread between them. They have decreased significantly and will simply, at some arbitrary moment, stop. Worse, there's no line of conversation that will interrupt this sequence of events. Lacy has tried and given up. Shane is a Harlem Globetrotter with the ball of truth.

Lacy has moved into her own B-movie. Fatalism is all that's available to her now, fatalism and clichés. She spends most of her time on the chenille-covered bed, watching the neon sign flash off and on at three a.m. outside the venetian-blinded window of the cheap hotel in some Mexican border town of the soul.

She begins walking by Shane's house late at night. Sometimes there's a note stuck between the door and the frame. These are folded-over pieces of paper with YVETTE scrawled on the outside. Yvette lives downstairs from Shane. Lacy sometimes unfolds and reads these messages, and takes comfort in the fact that someone is in more trouble over Yvette than Lacy is over Shane. She might walk by here at three in the morning, might look to see if there are lights on upstairs, but she's a ways off from long, crazed messages scribbled on pages ripped out of her address book.

One night, she loses it. She presses the doorbell, but although there are dim lights on, no one responds. Like someone in a cheap trance, a character in a horror movie of the fifties where the island natives are turning the tourists into zombies, she goes around and up the back stairs. As she approaches the landing outside Shane's apartment, the light in the kitchen flicks off. This doesn't even slow her step. When she gets to the back door, she presses her nose into the screen and peers through it.

Shane is there, standing stock still in the dark, looking straight back at Lacy, close enough that Lacy can hear her breathing.

As Lacy walks back down the stairs, she tries to imagine a time in the far distant future when she will be able to think back on this moment without humiliation. Maybe when she's ninety, a tapestry of experience woven behind her, everything in perspective and constant pain from arthritis making everything else seem insignificant. But probably not even then.

As soon as the pool is finished, Mrs. Crooks begins spending a lot of her time in it. Her pink plaid two-piece bathing suit makes no concessions to her figure. The bra part contains barely half of her enormous breasts. The snarling head and dice-shaking tail of the snake tattoo peek out at different places. Her stomach drapes in folds over the bikini bottom, a large operation scar in white relief. But she's comfortable with her body; if someone else isn't, it's their problem.

She's getting quite tan. A serious tanner, she lies out only during prime time, wears eye cups and a bandana. She uses cream with a mid-level sun-protection factor. She's concerned about aging effects.

She's learning to swim. Instead of goggles, she wears her regular glasses, held on with a sports strap. She takes out her teeth. She clips on a nose plug, wears flippers and a life belt. She does everything but take out insurance.

She started to teach herself from a book she got at the library. Lacy came out one morning and saw her in the water, holding the book aloft with one hand, trying with the other to duplicate the stroke in the illustration. Since then Lacy gives her twice-a-week lessons. And Mrs. Crooks is improving; she's not drowning her way across the pool anymore. She's still astoundingly slow, though, like a flower blooming in time-lapse photography. Today she's doing something wildly creative with the breast stroke.

"How am I doing?" she splutters as she gets to the edge where Lacy is sitting and grabs onto her calves.

"I don't think I've seen that kick before," Lacy says.

"It's in the book. It's supposed to go with the side stroke. How're you doing? You look really terrible."

Lacy pulls up the pool thermometer by its plastic cord.

"Eighty-two," she says.

"You don't tell me your troubles because you think I hate this lezbo stuff. But I'm getting better. Now I just don't like her for your sake. You look like a ham and egger in the fourteenth round. If she's going to take you out with a left hook, I just wish she'd land it and be done."

"Yes. That would probably be better than this, waiting to know that it's really over. Finally."

Mrs. Crooks paddles over to the chrome ladder and hoists herself up, a rush of water cascading down her back as she emerges. She gets her towel and wraps it around her waist, then sits down next to Lacy. She picks her teeth up off the cement and pops them in, sucking and tongueing them into place.

"Did you ever notice how they don't make a goodbye Candygram?" she says. "You're such a dope. You think if there's an ending, it's got to have big music so someone knows to turn the lights up. Most people just take a hike. Listen for the door shutting behind them. That's all the farewell you're going to get. Like me. I pick up my stuff, move on, and don't look back."

*And look where it got you,* Lacy thinks. Mrs. Crooks hears the thought.

"I realize that as a game plan, it has its limitations. Of course, it doesn't happen all at once. You break off your connections, and then there's no one to turn to. You get a cold and stay home from work for a while, but then you don't ever quite feel like going back again. You move out of one place, into another, and then another. And then there comes a move where you move out, but you don't move in. Maybe you start living out of your car. So much simpler. No muss, no fuss. And then one day the car dies and you hear this tiny 'snip' behind you, and you know the last string's been cut. You're floating free."

Lacy reaches down and rumples Mrs. Crooks's hair, or rather something just shy of rumpling, given that she has only punky chick fluff on top.

"I put you down as my Most Admired Woman on the questionnaire for the *People* poll," Mrs. Crooks tells her.

Lacy, already wobbly with her own tragedy, is so moved by this that she begins to cry. Mrs. Crooks pats her knee wetly.

"Don't. I changed it at the last minute to Oprah. I had to be practical. It's going to be tight between her and Mother Teresa."

L acy comes down with the flu, or something. Whatever it is, she gets a horrible case of it, and the company in her house only makes it worse.

Franco is terrible around illness. His imagination bounds. On the first bad day, while Lacy is sleeping terribly up and down the dragstrip of fever, he comes in and begins to administer the last rites.

"What's this?" she says, mistaking the anointing oil. "Chapstick?"

"Extreme unction."

"Honey, I don't want to seem ungrateful, but..."

"I'm almost finished."

She asks him to stay downstairs for a few days. This is better, but she can still hear him droning a nearly incessant stream of litanies, begging God to spare her.

"So young," she hears him telling Harry on the phone. "So full of promise."

Mrs. Crooks is another kind of awful. She believes that what's ailing Lacy is the grippe, and has expedients to wrestle this old nemesis to the mat. She cooks up a pot of garlic syrup, and mixes a mustard plaster to spread on Lacy's chest.

"What you want is to draw the poisons out. Through the pores is best."

Lacy locks her door.

A day later, maybe two—it's hard for her to keep track through the worst of it—Shane is there, the childhood fantasy come true. *They treat me mean, but won't they all be sorry when I get real sick. Then they'll be so nice.*

But in coming true when she's thirty-seven instead of seven, the fantasy is sullied, fresh snow with footprints already marking it by the time she wakes up. The prints are her worry that Shane has been bribed into this appearance by an appeal to her pity, lured here by some grim picture Franco has painted. She doesn't ask, though. She's too weak.

Shane peels Lacy's sweaty T-shirt and underpants off, puts her into a lukewarm tub, rubs her afterward with lotion, puts her into a fresh T-shirt and underpants and pops her back into bed. She calls a doctor, takes notes on a pad, then is gone. Then is back with pills and an orange slush.

"It's got a flexi-straw," she says, softly pushing it into Lacy's mouth. "Nobody doesn't like a flexi-straw."

When Lacy's awake, Shane plays CDs for her on the stereo. While Lacy sleeps, Shane sits in a chair pulled up by the bed, and writes her dopey messages with a beginner's calligraphy set she bought at the drugstore. When Lacy wakes up again, Shane pulls off both their clothes and climbs in beside her, holds her through the night.

The illness creates a dispensation. This doesn't count. It's a free-floating epilogue with no strings attached. And so for a couple of days, Shane can love her plainly, and Lacy can have a piece of fearlessness.

By dusk of the second day, Lacy has come through the fever. Shane scrambles them some eggs and heats up some frozen blueberry muffins, brews a pot of tea, then cleans up the kitchen while Lacy sits in a bath reading a *Weekly World News* Shane bought for her. After the bath, Shane washes Lacy's hair and blows it dry, moussing it up into a Tina Turner special.

"This is a real corporeal work of mercy," Lacy says.

"Nah. It's fun. You can do it for me if I get sick." Implying a future.

"Of course," Lacy says, conspiring with the lie, fooling around with finality. The flu makes her philosophical. She has a brief moment of accepting that loving Shane is like loving the Venus de Milo. She has to go with what's there. It would be no good wishing for arms too.

Shane says goodbye as though she's just going to work, although they both know she's not coming back.

That night is, oddly, all right. The next day is dreadful, though; the night, worse. Lacy sits through to dawn on a chaise by the pool, wrapped in a cotton blanket. She imagines herself old, English, on shipboard. Virginia Woolf crossing to Calais. Sometime just before dawn, she begins to think it probably wasn't even really love. Just a reckless extravagance of gesture with not much backing it up. Like spending lire.

Bounding into the next day on no sleep, she decides to put a few miles between her and this island. She gets in the Camaro and heads up to the mainland. At Marathon, she runs head-on into a storm. She barely has time to pull over and get the top up. The rest of the way is rough going with the rain punishing the canvas above her head, crashing across bridges, bending palms to its will. At Islamorada, the storm and the surf blur, and she's nearly washed off the road. Her mood filters fear into exhilaration. Instead of feeling at odds with these elements, she feels as though she's on a roll with them.

In Miami she stalks through a mall, buying recklessly with money the Visa company doesn't know she doesn't have.

Presents to buy happiness for everyone. A dozen oldies CDs for Franco. A huge Japanese satin robe for Mrs. Crooks. A silk drawstring bag for Heather. For herself, baggy linen shorts, purple high-top tennis shoes.

The storm has broken by the time she comes out of the mall. The palms are still dripping, and Fed One is awash in a few places on the way down. But in the sky, all the traces have been kicked over. The setting sun is pouring orange onto the gulf.

When she gets home, Mrs. Crooks is on the front sun porch, typing horoscopes on a Smith-Corona portable that belonged to Lacy's father at Dartmouth.

"How's this do you think?" she says to Lacy, who is bringing in the first bunch of packages.

DO IT JUST TO SPITE THEM. YOU'LL FEEL BETTER.

"Who's them?" Lacy says.

"Oh, everybody's got a 'them.' Where've you been?"

"Miami. I got us all presents. I'll go get Franco."

"He left a note on the door while I was out." She pulls it from the breast pocket of her bowling shirt, which has CEDRIC embroidered in script above it. Lacy can't imagine anyone both being named Cedric and bowling.

The note says, "Come up. Something wonderful has happened."

The message has a little subtext. In the right upper corner there's a thumb smudge of dried blood.


She sets the packages down on the glider and tries to hear her thoughts over the hammering in her ears.

When she gets to his door, she knocks, hoping he'll answer brightly and the wonderful thing will be that a couple who met on *Love Connection,* a couple he was rooting for, got married. But she knows this won't be the wonderful thing. She knows what it is, and that he won't answer the door, that she's going to have to go in and see it.

The room is closed-up, the shutters pulled in against the storm, the air hot and orangy from the incense and the candles—at least a hundred are lit. The place is thick with ritual. It's like a ceremonial cave.

He's in bed, on the far side of the altar, which has the Roy Orbison monstrance displayed atop the tabernacle. She hasn't seen this out for years. He's not asleep, but looks a little trancy. He sees Lacy and smiles, and he is truly radiant. Beatific. He holds out his hands for her to see. The holes are small, neat punctures, not gaping wounds. Blood is seeping out of them in the thinnest, slowest imaginable lines. She becomes suddenly and violently ill. She feels as though she's looping back into the fever. She slumps into a rattan chair at the foot of the bed, drops her head between her knees, presses her palms to the cool stony floor.

When she's able to sit up again, he's asleep, on his side, hands pressed between drawn-up knees. She watches him for a while, and tries to mobilize her thoughts. She's not sure who to call—doctor, priest, shrink. She ultimately defaults to doctor. The only one who comes to mind is the guy Shane called for her the other day. Hagen. She calls his office, is put on hold by a receptionist, and sits with the receiver to her ear through "Guantanamera" and "Do You Know the Way to San Jose?" which Dr. Hagen breaks into abruptly.

Lacy can't think of how to even begin with the truth, and so lies and says her fever has flared up again. She works at sounding hallucinatory, and eventually persuades him to come by on his way home.

When he arrives, Lacy's waiting for him outside. He roars up on a motorcycle, unstraps his black bag from behind the seat.

"So," he says.

"It's not me, really. It's my brother."

As she's leading him in, she has a brief flash of hope that she imagined the whole thing, that on the other side of the door, Franco will be napping—normally, his hands closed up like everyone else's.

But no. He is awake, out of bed, circling the altar with the incense canister, flipping it toward the monstrance, genuflecting in between, dripping blood as he goes.

E verett, the place in Miami where Dr. Hagen has sent Franco for "observation," doesn't look like a nuthouse. It's not so much one building as a cluster of low, motel-like pastel stucco structures attached to each other at odd angles. Coming up the drive, it looks like it could be a health spa, a corporate conference center.

Nothing snakepitty ever seems to be going on when Lacy visits. No screams from within. No one hanging by his belt. There are usually a lot of patients out on the heavily land-scaped lawns, and from a distance, they don't even seem crazy; they just move around with less or more direction than the general population.

Closer up, the atmosphere breaks down into slightly more unsettling specifics. A plump, middle-aged woman coming toward Lacy is suddenly walking alongside her. She identifies herself as Dan Rather.

Others are talking to themselves. There are a few Thora-zined tongues creeping out of the corners of mouths. Still, the crowd is not really much worse than on a particularly ripe night along Duval.

Each building or wing is a different pastel color. Lacy thinks there's probably a code, but hasn't cracked it yet. Franco is in Green, but she doesn't know if it would be better if he were in Blue, worse if he were in Tan.

He has been here three weeks. She has been here three times, but this is the first time she's being allowed to visit him. The first two times she was allowed only to talk with—or rather be talked at by—Dr. Bellows, a psychiatrist colleague of Hagen, who has taken up Franco's case. Lacy's impressions of Bellows are that he is young and earnest, and in way over his head with Franco.

He's confident, though. He tells her that Franco is progressing well, responding to medication. The wounds are healing up. He is much less religiously hysterical, less obsessed, less depressively ironic in his worldview. Bellows says Franco is doing well in socializing with other patients, and excelling in the crafts workshop. There was initially a small problem, some confusion over his output of trivets made from tongue depressors. Apparently he thought he was on a quota system, and was making fifty a day until it was explained to him that this activity was in the nature of a hobby.

Although the TV minicams of her nightmares have not arrived, Lacy gets the impression that there's considerable interest in Franco around here, that the observation is as much for the careers of the observers as for the good of the observed. Someone has flown in from Germany, a specialist in "this sort of phenomena," as Bellows puts it. He's vague about the German, and what he's doing with Franco. The basic policy toward relatives here seems to be O&M. Obfuscation and mollification.

She's no longer at all sure she did the right thing. Franco's stigmata does not seem to be self-inflicted. Perhaps it was somehow psychologically induced, but what if it was simply received—the gift he has been waiting so long for—and her response to this high point of his life has been to lock him up?

Lacy listens to Bellows, then thinks between his lines, and by now is pretty sure that what the German has in mind is suspending Franco in a sterile solution, pipette-ing him up and into a petri dish, then keeping good notes on what happens from there. She's pretty sure that what Bellows has in mind is "getting Franco well," which translates as turning Franco into a veal cutlet.

Mrs. Crooks insists on coming along this time. She wants to see the place for herself. ("I've a little experience in this area.") And she has presents for Franco—a can of sardines in mustard, a packet of Garfield stationery, some religious comics from the fifties featuring a missionary brother with superpowers.

When they're almost to the front door, Lacy notices for the first time that Mrs. Crooks has done her version of dressing up for the visit. She's wearing some brown stirrup pants that make her stomach look like a kangaroo pouch, a shirt that's shiny and patterned and of a material quite far removed from nature, an import from another dimension. She takes Lacy's stare as appreciation.

"I dressed up a little. You want to be careful when you go to these places. Sometimes they decide you look more like a patient than a visitor and next thing you know they've slid the bar across the gates and it's Frances Farmer time. They strap you to the old table and run a few jillion jolt volts through you. Straighten you out. You know those treatments—most people don't know this—if you go in with curly hair, it comes out straight. You go in with straight hair, it comes out curly."

They find Franco sitting in a lawn chair out behind the green building. He is putting on a little weight, getting a little sunburned. He's wearing old khakis and a Hawaiian shirt Lacy doesn't recognize. His hands have small bandages on them. He looks quite healthy. He's reading a biography of Harry Houdini. He doesn't seem surprised to see them.

"What a mausoleum," Mrs. Crooks says, looking around at all the pastel and lawn and calm. She offers her gifts, waits for Franco to appreciate them, gives him a peering once-over, then says she's going to check the place out.

"Already I can tell you, though, I've seen plenty worse."

When Mrs. Crooks has walked off, Lacy sits down on the grass in front of Franco and puts her hands on his knees.

"So. What's it like here?" she says.

"Full of crazy people."

"You know, they don't look too crazy, though. I was surprised."

"Well, they've been mellowed out. Pills. Shots. Treatments. They can click you from channel to channel depending on what they give you. This is the third—no, fourth—channel I've been on. I think everybody here in Green is on Channel Four. Except maybe Alvarez. He thinks this is a NASA training center. He thinks he's scheduled to go up on the next shuttle—that they don't want to risk blowing up any more school teachers and so they're sending mental patients no one cares about. I don't think they've been able to find a drug that stops him from being convinced he's an astronaut. You can tell he stumps them. They don't like that. They don't want any astronauts around here. That's sort of the point of the place."

"How are you feeling?" she says to him. "Better?"

He looks at her with such utter disappointment that she knows if he weren't so heavily medicated, it would be utter rage at her meddling. "You don't understand," he says. "I'll *never* feel better than I did when it happened. That was the best I'm going to get. There was a moment in there when the light, suddenly it was so bright, like a thousand flashbulbs. Popping like that too. But without any sound. It was like he was sending me a message."

"Like?"

"As far as I can tell, he's not a real chatty guy. I think he was just saying something like 'hey.'"

"What do you tell Bellows, and the German?"

"Oh, I have a lot of fun with them, especially Bellows. Doesn't he have a remarkable amount of hair in his ears? I mean, for a young guy?"

"You don't tell them about the popping lights?"

Franco doesn't dignify this with an answer.

"The interesting thing," he says, "is that to them, God's just another nuisance. He's in the same bin with ghosts and intergalactic aliens and Ricardo Montalban, who used to visit Mrs. Noonan here every night until they got her on Channel Four." He pauses for a moment, then says, "You shouldn't have called Hagen. He and Bellows are real morons."

"It seemed like a good idea at the time," Lacy says. "Well, it was the only idea I could come up with on such short notice."

"And now you're going to leave me here."

"Don't be silly."

"You think everything's gone out of whack, and it's beyond you and so you'll just leave me in the capable hands of professionals. Then run off with that stewardess in a gym teacher's body."

Lacy presses her forehead against his knee so he won't see her smile. The Houdini book slides off his lap onto the grass. He doesn't seem to notice. Lacy hands it back to him anyway. She thinks for a minute.

"Maybe we just need to rearrange the arrangement a little. I've been thinking. Maybe I haven't done you such a big favor, you know...picking up all the slack for you. It's probably been neurotic on my part. I mean, I love taking care of you, but probably too much. And it's probably kept you from..."

"Developing my potential to the fullest," he says flatly. His affect is way down. The medication, Lacy figures. It's eerie, like talking to Franco, but not quite Franco.

"Something like that," she says. " Maybe what you need now is..."

"Tough love," he says, sarcasm triumphing over major sedation. "Just think, if it works, we can probably go on *Donahue* and tell all about it."

"Please be serious."

"Lacy. Of *course* our relationship is neurotic. So what? It works."

She shakes her head.

"I don't want the whole weight of it anymore. You're just going to have to take some of it off me. I've loved you your whole life by letting you be you. Now you're going to have to return the gesture."

He doesn't say anything.

"Can you?"

"Maybe."

"I need to know."

"Tired," he says. "You get sleepy a lot from the shots. It's hard to fight all their systems at once. You have to fight so hard, and at the same time not let them see that you're fighting at all."

"Oh, honey," Lacy says. He stands up slowly and takes her hand. She walks with him toward the green building. Then she goes to see Bellows.

His office is small and has no window. It's painted white with one bright blue accent wall. His desk is piled high with deadly looking scholarly journals and piles of cigarette butts that probably have ashtrays somewhere beneath them.

"So, how's our boy?" he asks her now.

"How do you think he's doing?"

"Oh, fine, fine. Much improved. He's really opening up lately in our little sessions. Finally, after all that silence, it's all just spilling out. The years in Brazil. The indignity of your parents' profession."

"Yes, well that's good." Franco's been having a good time.

"The psychiatric literature on clowns is minimal, but I'm talking to a colleague in Sarasota. He works with some of the Ringling people."

"So how soon do you think my brother will be ready to come out?"

"Oh, let's not be hasty now," Bellows says and chuckles. Lacy wants to put a metal bucket over his head and bang on it with a hammer. Instead, she nods in what she hopes looks like a serious and deferential manner.

Mrs. Crooks is waiting in the car when Lacy gets there. She pulls a sample pack of cigarettes out of her carryall. She lights two, like Paul Henreid in *Now Voyager*, and passes one across the front seat to Lacy.

"Well," she says when she's ready, "I'm glad I got up here. He really appreciated those sardines, I can tell you."

"How did he seem to you?"

"He's going to take a correspondence course."

This is news to Lacy. "In what?"

"I can't recall."

"Please."

"Something to do with insurance. Undertaking."

"Underwriting."

"It's their idea. They want him to get his feet back on the ground. No more fooling around with that opera. They say that's just the sort of thing that loosens him up from reality."

"How do you know all this?"

"I slipped around and got a snitchy look at his file. Then I found the linen closet." She pulls out a short stack of pillow cases. PSYCHO is stenciled on the hem of each. "I can get us pajamas next time. The security here is shit."

"What else was in the file?"

"They've got him loaded up with lots of m-g's of something. They've been increasing it all along. They're flattening him out. Getting him nice and pancakey."

Sometime in the middle of the night, Lacy comes in from the backyard and sits on the edge of Mrs. Crooks's bed. Her eyes pop open immediately. A reflex action from years of wary nights in flophouses.

"We're going to have to get him out, aren't we?" Lacy says.

Mrs. Crooks looks at Lacy as if she's belaboring the obvious. "Go get some sleep."

But she can't. She goes out back and peels off her shorts and t-shirt. She tosses a raft into the nightblack water of the pool and dives in after it. She slides on and lies naked in the pale moonlight, drifting silently for a long while, trying to think meticulously, in tiny reasonable steps.

With a whoosh, although there's no actual sound, the underwater lights come on beneath her. It's Shane. She steps out of the darkness and sits on the lip of the pool. For some reason, Lacy isn't all that surprised to see her. She just stays in the middle, ruddering with tiny little underwater flips of her hands.

Shane slides into the water with her clothes on. She submerges and swims underwater, coming up next to Lacy, pulling her silently off the raft. When she kisses her, her whole mouth is cold, even inside. From the water.

Lacy lets it happen.

"I heard," Shane says. "Claudia told me." Something about the way Shane says "Claudia" makes Lacy know she's been sleeping with her, that it was Claudia behind the partially closed bathroom door that day.

"It's bad up there," Lacy says. "We're going to try to get him out."

"Won't you get in trouble?"

"I'll take him away for a while. In case they come looking."

"I'll wait here."

"Shane. Try to have a conscience. Don't jack this up just for the sake of a little late-night drama."

"But I want to try. I've been thinking. I can be a better version of me."

"I don't want to do this anymore. Really. It's making me a person I don't like."

"Please," Shane says and after a long time of the word hanging in the air between them, Lacy takes Shane's hand underwater.

"Come inside. There's something I want to show you."

She gets them both towels and fresh shorts and T-shirts and then takes Shane into the studio. Lacy flips on the overhead lights and, for the first time, shows her private paintings to another person. And for once Shane doesn't play dumb. She sees that the paintings are all, in various ways, about her.

"Boy," she says and sits down on the yellow sofa. Then, "You know, if I were you, I wouldn't show these to me."

"Oh, I'm way beyond strategy. It's much more crucial that you understand how ridiculously important this has become to me. It's too much to put me through anymore. It's not decent. I'm sort of fast on my feet, and maybe that makes me seem sophisticated or something. But I'm not. Basically I've spent the past years hanging out with my brother and painting and looking at girls. I haven't been practicing for you. I don't have any defenses against you or mechanisms for getting through you. For you this is a way of being clever, some kind of romantic wittiness. I can't do that. I'll always be taking it seriously. I won't be any fun at all."

"I'm more serious than you think."

Lacy doesn't say anything.

"Give me a key to the house. I'll take your mail in while you're gone. Water your plants. It'll give us a connection. Something symbolic. And when you come back, I'll hear you coming and be waiting when you come through the door."

"Oh, God." Lacy says and closes her eyes and can already see the magazines and envelopes scattered on the floor just inside the door, the plants yellow and brown and brittle.

"Do you think they're any good?" she asks, gesturing at the canvases propped around the room.

"Oh yeah," Shane says, but as soon as she's said it, Lacy doesn't know why she even bothered to ask. Shane is so vain she might like potholders appliquéd with her picture.

"Help me get them crated," Lacy says. "Before I lose my nerve. Tomorrow after I've gone, take them to Harry. Tell him to do what he can." She gets up and heads for the bathroom. She suddenly has a crushing headache. Shane follows and waits and watches and chins herself on the doorframe. Lacy finds the ibuprofen and takes three, then says into the mirror, "It wasn't even love, was it? Not even at the beginning?"

Shane drops from the door frame, then comes and turns Lacy around. Wiping the water off her mouth, she clamps big hands on Lacy's shoulders.

"Look. Let's get the story straight. You weren't looking for someone reasonable. Some horn-rimmed person with sensible shoes—you'd save up together to go on a budget walking tour of Scotland together. I knew women like that in Boston. Not your type. You came looking for me. Exactly me. So now don't turn around and go into all this despair because I turned out to be exactly what you wanted. On the dot. And don't give me any more of that bogus bullshit about it not being love. Asshole," she says, pulling Lacy out of her clothes, and down onto the cool tile floor.

After she's gone, Lacy packs through what little is left of the night. At dawn, she drives over to the houseboat of one of the lightly dangerous guys she went with when she first moved back onto the island. He is in the business of identity adjustment. For two hundred dollars, he sells her a pair of Florida plates.

At nine, she calls Bellows and tells him that she and Franco's Aunt Iris want to come and take him out to Wendy's for lunch. Bellows has mentioned outings, so Lacy knows they are a possibility. After an unnervingly long pause, he says all right, so long as they make only the one stop and are back within the hour.

"Often," he says, "the first time outside is rather over-whelming, so we try to make these excursions simple. Short and not too stimulating."

Lacy asks if it might be wiser to take him just to the McDonald's. It's two blocks closer to the hospital. Dr. Bellows gives this some consideration, but eventually says that if Franco prefers Wendy's, the two extra blocks will probably be okay.

"Better not come until after one or so," he adds. "I see on Franco's schedule that he's expecting some other visitors this morning."

Lacy can't imagine who this could be, but doesn't want to jeopardize her plan with any more conversation.

At nine-thirty, she locks the front door and gets in the Camaro. Mrs. Crooks is already waiting in the back seat. She's in full travel regalia. Sun visor and shades with a little clip-on rearview mirror attached. She's wearing floppy Bermudas, high-top purple tennis shoes and her LIFE'S A BEACH T-shirt.

Just before they hit Marathon, a wave of something—something to the side of sadness—comes over Lacy. She has no idea where they'll be going, when they'll come back; they can't come back to the same life they're leaving behind. She cries across all seven miles of the Seven Mile Bridge. Somehow, it seems a metaphorical point of no return. Mrs. Crooks, who has been asleep since Stock Island, misses this milestone.

They pull into the parking lot at Everett. Mrs. Crooks waits in the car while Lacy goes to find Franco.

On the main path, she passes two guys talking agitatedly over a phone-book–sized manuscript they're holding between them. They look amazingly like Mick Jagger and Keith Richards. Delusional, she thinks. It's not until several minutes later that she realizes the delusion would be hers.

She finally finds Franco in the recreation center, watching a Ping Pong game between an elderly Asian man and a young guy with a ponytail.

Lacy goes over and takes Franco by the hand, pulls him up out of his chair.

"Come on. We're going for a cheeseburger."

"Oh," he says, seeming quite a ways off from being able to grab the rope. "I think I already had lunch."

Lacy turns and stares hard at him. It's a while before he smiles, as if he had to pull the smile out of some dusty recess.

"Ah," he says. "You are referring to the cosmic cheeseburger."

On their way out of the lot, the security guard has Lacy mark the sign-out sheet. She fills in three p.m. as time of return, while he goes around and takes down the number of a license plate she'll change at the first rest area.

Once they're on their way, Franco wants to know where they're heading.

"I haven't taken this very far," Lacy says. "I guess we're just sort of lighting out for the territory."

He's ecstatic, which is understandable. Less understandable to Lacy is her own ecstasy, which doesn't seem very warranted by barreling toward the void in a beater Chevy.

From the back seat, a windswept Mrs. Crooks, who even in the midst of leaving needs to be leaving, says, "You know, I'll probably just ride with you kids as far as Atlanta."